Extraordinary

Extraordinary

By Dawn Knox

Bridge House

British Library Cataloguing in Publication Data
A Record of this Publication is available from the British Library

ISBN 978-1-907335-51-8

This edition published 2017 by Bridge House Publishing
Manchester, England

All Bridge House books are published on paper derived from sustainable resources.

Dedication

To Mum, Jamie and James.
Thank you for believing in me.
To Dad.
I miss you and think of you every day.

Contents

Introduction

These stories – some light and some dark – were written over several years. A few, such as *Henry's Box*, were the result of writing prompts from one of my writing groups, Basildon Writers, while others were sparked by random sights, such as someone's tattoo, or by snatches of overheard conversation. As for the rest, I can't recall any particular event triggering them, so can only conclude the initial idea popped into my head when I wasn't paying attention. And sometimes I find those sort of stories turn out to be the strangest of them all. Whether you prefer light or dark stories, I hope there is something amongst this eclectic collection that will appeal to you.

Dawn Knox

Earthrights

'Now, tell me, exactly why are you selling the rights to Earth?' said the Chossey.

Bohnan sighed.

He'd already explained the reason in great detail but the Chossey didn't seem to be the brightest spark in the inferno. And to be honest, it was just as well. This deal was important and he didn't want a potential buyer to work out the drawbacks before he signed.

He'd schemed for months and it wouldn't do to lose patience now.

Bohnan the Carbairian smiled winningly with both mouths, gritted his fangs and started again.

'I'm getting old. I want to retire. I have a little holiday home in the Drosophila Galaxy and I'd like to end my days there.'

'The *what* Galaxy?'

'Drosophila.'

'Never heard of it'

'It's not very well known at the moment but it's a very up-and-coming location. Property prices are set to rocket. If you're interested, I know of a very desirable little place not far from mine.'

'Really?' said the Chossey, his single eye lighting up with excitement, 'Yes, I would be interested.'

'But I digress,' said Bohnan quickly, 'there's plenty of time to discuss holiday homes after we've settled the ownership of the Earth,' he smiled encouragingly with both mouths.

Steady on old chap, thought Bohnan. *There'll be plenty of time to sell him property in an imaginary galaxy later.*
He just needed the Chossey to sign on the dotted line and then... then, he'd head to the furthest reaches of the

9

universe and live out the rest of his days in luxury.

'You don't look old enough to retire.'

Bohnan paused for a second. Had he underestimated the Chossey? Was he attempting to smooth the deal with flattery? Or worse, was he suspicious?

The blank expression on the Chossey's face suggested that neither explanation was the case. He was like a terrestrial dog with a bone, Bohnan finally decided, he simply hadn't quite absorbed Bohnan's reason for selling the rights and was merely trying to make sense of it all. The act of information processing was painful to watch, but he reminded himself that the Chossey's stupidity should work to his advantage.

'It's not so much that I'm old,' he began, 'but I'm *feeling* old. You know how it is. Some days it's a struggle to get out of bed. I'm tired and I long for some rest. And then again, there's my war wound,' he said, rubbing his scaly thigh.

The Chossey nodded sympathetically.

Bohnan pressed on 'And that's why I want to sell the rights to the Earth.'

'But you don't exactly own the Earth yet, do you?' said the Chossey.

Bohnan had anticipated this – even the Chossey would have noticed that he hadn't yet staged his invasion of the Blue Planet.

'I've lost interest,' he said casually 'I prefer the chase to the kill but I've done the necessary preparation and all that now remains is for someone bold and brave, such as yourself, to walk in and take over.'

The Chossey licked his blubbery lips in anticipation.

'Mankind is now in such a weakened state that they'll be unable to resist an attack,' continued Bohnan.

'How d'you know they're so weak?'

'Because I weakened them.'

'How?'

'That's part of the deal. I explain how the human race has been completely undermined and how you can claim the Earth's riches... and you pay me three million Goron ducats.'

If the Chossey had possessed an eyebrow, it would undoubtedly have shot upwards towards his hairline. As it was, the single eye opened so wide, it was in danger of popping out.

'Th-three million?'

Bohnan fought back laughter. He'd happily settle for one million but the Chossey had to believe that what he was offering was priceless.

'No,' said the Chossey 'you're asking too much. No planet's worth that, especially one that's overcrowded with revolting human beings and is full of disgusting water'.

'Without giving too much of my secret away, that's the beauty of it.'

'What? Human beings and water?' asked the Chossey.

'Exactly. The wealth on that planet is incalculable. Trust me, I've been watching the humans for countless Earth years.'

'I know,' said the Chossey smugly, 'we've been watching *you* watch *them*.'

'Have you?' said Bohnan in mock surprise.

He knew exactly who was observing him at any given moment and had detected the clumsy surveillance of the Chossey. Interestingly, the objects of his examination, the humans, were completely unaware of his presence or the fact that they'd been monitored for years.

His performance of astonishment at being observed had fooled the Chossey, whose fleshy lips were drawn sideways into such a wide grin, they looked like they were in danger

11

of bursting. Bohnan had the overwhelming urge to reach across and slap the stupid, self-satisfied smirk from his face. With great restraint, he resisted and instead, scratched at the scaly creases in his neck. Small insects scuttled out of the deep crevices and darted about in panic over the rough, reptilian skin, looking for sanctuary. Bohnan seized one of the creatures between two claws and studied it absent-mindedly.

'Mankind is as vulnerable as this...' he said as he exerted a fraction more pressure on the creature's carapace. The crunch was scarcely audible.

With fore-claw and thumb, he flicked the remnants of the unfortunate bug into the air and wiped his paw down the front of his stained vest.

A cruel gleam lit up the Chossey's eye.

'As easy to crush as that, eh?'

'Easier.' Bohnan slid the contract across the desk.

The Chossey picked up the pen.

Bohnan held his breath. Surely he wouldn't be foolish enough to sign without reading it? But there was always hope.

'How?' asked the Chossey.

'How what?'

'How can they be crushed?'

'You simply land on Earth and take over. There'll be no resistance – I can guarantee that. Then you simply help yourself to the resources. As I said, the humans will surrender without a fight.'

The Chossey glanced up at the ceiling with a faraway look in his eye.

He's hooked, thought Bohnan and held his breath again.

'No,' said the Chossey sharply, 'no, the price is too high and I need more information.'

'We can come to some sort of arrangement, I'm sure.'

It's time to exert a little pressure, thought Bohnan and casually moving his hand under the desk, he pressed a small button.

'Yes, I'm sure we can come to a mutually, satisfactory agreement,' he said as a sequence of rapid bleeps rang out.

'Excuse me, please,' said Bohnan, turning a knob on the console on his desk.

On the far side of the wooden-panelled room, concealed doors slid apart silently, revealing a screen which clicked, blinked and lit up.

'Bohnan, my old friend…' the face that had spoken, broke up into a series of lines and zig-zags but the voice was still audible. 'I hear you're selling the rights to Earth. Don't accept any offers before I get there! I'm just leaving the Drosophila Galaxy – I'll be with you soon.'

'Harlix! How good to hear your voice…hello…Harlix? Harlix?' said Bohnan, 'damn, he's gone…'

'Bad signal,' commented the Chossey, who had picked up the pen again. 'How long before he arrives?'

Bohnan breathed a silent sigh of relief. The Chossey had fallen for it. He really believed that his ancient rival, Harlix, was on his way and was interested in buying Earth.

It hadn't taken Bohnan long to mock up the communication using a clip of an earlier call from Harlix and then a voice simulator to produce the message and it'd certainly been worth the effort.

'Would you accept one million Goron ducats?'

Bohnan chewed his thumb thoughtfully and pretended to consider the offer.

'I was hoping for a bit more than that. Perhaps we ought to wait until Harlix arrives and see what sort of offer he makes.'

'Two million. I can't go higher than that.'

'Done,' said Bohnan quickly, making the Chossey jump. 'Sign here.'

The Chossey seemed rather bewildered by the speed at which Bohnan had agreed, and he hesitated.

'Here,' said Bohnan tapping the contract with his fore-claw, 'and here.'

The Chossey laboriously signed the paper twice and looked up.

'Now. I want to know how you weakened the humans.'

'I'll tell you everything, when I've seen the ducats.'

The Chossey withdrew a large pouch from his baggy coat and tipped the contents on to the desk.

'One million,' he said.

Bohnan banged his fist on the desk.

'We agreed two million!'

'You don't expect me to carry around such large sums, do you? I'm not that stupid!'

Bohnan had scanned the Chossey when he'd come aboard the ship and knew that he had two money pouches in his coat. He seized the contract and pretended he was about to tear it up.

'I knew I ought to have waited for Harlix,' he said regretfully.

'Wait! I've just remembered. I brought out a little extra cash this morning.'

The Chossey reached into the other side of his shapeless coat and extracted another large bag. He tipped the contents on to the pile of coins on the desk.

Bohnan laid the contract down and swept the money towards him.

'Now,' he said with a self-satisfied smile, 'I'll tell you what I've been up to for the last few years. After much research, I've discovered that water, mixed with human fat can be converted to fuel.'

The Chossey gasped 'No!'

'Yes, it's true. There's a whole planet of humans just waiting to be converted to fuel.'

'How?' asked the Chossey, his eye wide with excitement.

'Here's the formula,' said Bohnan, sliding a large, fat, sealed packet across the desk 'but it'll take a while to read, so best save it for later,' he added as the Chossey started to open it.

'Not that the method is complicated,' Bohnan added quickly as the Chossey frowned and looked doubtfully at the envelope, 'there's just quite a lot to read, that's all.'

The Chossey would find out soon enough that the pages were filled with chemical symbols and scientific formulae that had absolutely nothing to do with fat or fuel but let him do that in his own time.

The Chossey placed the information in his pocket and patted it.

'So, how d'you get the fat out of the humans?'

'Just squeeze,' said Bohnan, 'humans crush remarkably easily.'

'How do you get rid of the blood and other stuff?'

'There's such a high proportion of fat, compared to the rest of the body that you don't need to take any special measures. Just press a human, allow the resulting 'soup' to settle and skim off the fat. Simple.'

The Chossey nodded with approval.

'Squeeze, settle and skim,' said Bohnan.

'But what happens when the humans run out?' asked the Chossey.

'That need never happen, if you manage them correctly.'

'Correctly?'

'Yes, you just need to establish fat farms.'

'Fat farms?'

Again, Bohnan had the almost uncontrollable urge to slap the vacant look off the Chossey's face and stop the echo. He moved slightly, jogging the desk and the ducats clinked together, reminding him that he would soon be free... and fabulously rich.

He made an effort to relax.

'Yes, fat farms,' he said through clenched fangs, 'to breed fat humans.'

'But you would need so many humans to make it cost effective,' said the Chossey.

'Ah!' said Bohnan; 'if you'd been observing the humans closely over the last few years, you'd know...' he held his breath, hoping that in fact, the Chossey hadn't been watching Earth.

'Go on...' said the Chossey.

Bohnan breathed a sigh of relief – obviously he hadn't been monitoring them.

'Well, if you'd been looking, you'd know what sort of shape the human race was in.'

He opened a drawer, withdrew a photograph that he'd previously cut from the *Universal Guinness Book of Records* and slid it across the desktop. He'd carefully removed the caption – Earth's Fattest Man and Woman.

'They're huge!' gasped the Chossey, staring in fascination. 'And that's...,' he said, pointing to the distended, sagging flesh.

Bohnan nodded with satisfaction, 'Yes, that's fat.'

'Are all the humans that size?' The Chossey's eye was large and round.

'No,' said Bohnan, 'these are just small ones. Mostly humans are bigger.'

The Chossey gasped as his mind played with the possibility of all the fuel that he'd be able to make.

'How did you grow them to that size?' he asked, shaking his head in amazement.

'That's the beauty of it. They do it all by themselves.'

Bohnan leaned back in his chair, folded his claws across his chest and smiled smugly.

The Chossey shook his head in awe, 'Simply ingenious...'

Bohnan allowed himself the luxury of basking in the glory for several seconds, then abruptly, he scooped up the pile of Goron ducats, deposited them in a leather pouch, which he dropped with a jingle of coins into his coat pocket.

He offered the Chossey his paw, 'Well, it's not often you can say that you gave someone the World and really mean it.'

'Sold someone the World, you mean.'

Bohnan shrugged. 'I'd hate to delay you any longer. I expect you're keen to investigate your new investment and start the squeezing. I'm quite keen to get away on holiday myself...'

'Ah yes, you said you'd let me know about that prime piece of property...'

'I'll be in touch,' said Bohnan curtly, herding the Chossey towards the door.

The escape plan had been conceived many months ago and by the time the Chossey realised that Bohnan wasn't aboard the decoy vessel travelling to the Tyrraenic Empire, he would be safely speeding past Capella, towards the outer reaches of the Auriga Galaxy. Two million ducats would buy him anonymity and a life of unimaginable luxury. Goron currency was highly prized by Aurigans, who were renowned for minding their own business – especially when offered some loose change in recompense. Anyway, it would take the Chossey a while to discover that humans were not all as large as Bohnan had led him to believe. That is, if he managed to land at all. There'd been several attempts to colonise Earth and they'd all been met with ferocious resistance. Humans might be ugly, smooth-skinned creatures but they were vicious when roused.

Not my problem, thought Bohnan, as he set his course for the Aurigan Galaxy, both mouths whistling in harmony.

The Game

Every picture tells a story, so they say.

Greer inspected the puzzle pieces, checking the image on each, trying to find a pattern, a sequence... some clue as to how the individual parts fitted into the whole. He carefully smoothed them out on the scarred, wooden table until their curling edges lay flat.

The legs of the once elegant table had been kicked and scuffed by countless, careless feet, beneath what had once been a polished tabletop. But the surface had long since succumbed to the cigarette burns, the drips and spills of beer cans and coffee mugs along with the many day to day insults that the countless tenants who had passed through this dreary room had inflicted upon it.

In its lifetime, the table had held aloft a surprising diversity of objects. Take, for example, the motor bike engine, which had once been stripped, cleaned and reassembled, or the amorous couple, who had eventually realised that the bed, although sagging, was a much better option for their passionate groping, or even the numerous fish, which had been gutted and descaled, leaving a faint aroma that was now part of the drab fabric of the room.

But never had the table borne witness to such a bizarre collection as this.

Greer frowned – this one was going to be tricky – probably the hardest puzzle he'd ever encountered, but he'd always succeeded before. Why should this one be any different?

He leaned over the table, rearranging the paper-thin pieces, examining the design on each. When he was satisfied with the layout, he limped to the stained hand basin in the corner of the room, grimacing as the knife wound in his thigh opened and began to bleed afresh. The

19

last scrap, drying on the shelf above the sink, had been the hardest to come by but he was certain from a brief inspection, that it was indeed the final portion of the puzzle. Acquiring that piece, he remembered, had almost led to his last moment…

The bulk of the leather-clad biker had belied his agility and Greer had realised almost too late that he'd completely underestimated his quarry. For five days, Greer had tailed the man, watching him come and go on his powerful motorbike. He'd seen him empty an unbelievable number of beer cans with other leather-clad bikers, devour staggering numbers of burgers and return occasionally to a squalid tenement block. By the end of the second day, Greer was certain this man possessed a piece of the puzzle and he strongly suspected it was the all-important final part, the only question now, was how to get it. The man followed no obvious routine like many of the others from whom Greer had seized puzzle pieces, so he could form no plan – his only option would be to snatch an opportunity at the first sign of vulnerability.

His chance came on the fifth night.

Greer saw the large biker stagger alone from the pub, swearing loudly for no apparent reason and at no one in particular. His legs, which appeared to be working independently of each other, steered him into a deserted, back street. Progress was slow and he yelled obscenities as he stumbled along the pavement, bouncing off the walls of the derelict warehouses accompanied by the echoes of his curses.

Easy pickings thought Greer, who was stalking him from the anonymity of the shadows but as he struck, the heavy man swerved nimbly blocking the garrotte with his fist, pulling a stiletto knife from who knew where.

Perhaps the frosty, night air had sobered him slightly or

perhaps he had some sort of sixth sense but within a second of striking, Greer knew he was in trouble.

Bellowing with rage, the biker stabbed blindly at his unseen attacker staggering forwards until he'd pinned Greer to the wall of the warehouse, using the considerable weight of his body. The force with which he'd been propelled into the wall, winded Greer, almost knocking him out and in desperation, he hung on to the garrotte, silently exhorting it to bite into his opponent's throat. It was now his only hope.

But the man had obviously underestimated Greer as well. He'd momentarily taken his hand from the garrotte, allowing Greer to tighten it around his neck and heave with all his strength.

The man began to claw frenziedly at the wire, trying to prise it from his throat but it had already started to slice into the folds of flabby flesh. His shouts became muted, strangled grunts as he struggled for breath and in a last desperate attempt to free himself, he slashed backwards with the knife. It struck the wall, clattering to the pavement but not before its blade had slashed Greer's thigh. With a sharp kick to the back of the biker's knees, Greer threw him off balance and managed to tighten the garrotte round the oversized neck, grunting with exertion as he tried to pull the wire through skin and cartilage – his boot in the small of the man's back, to give him leverage.

And just as he was beginning to fear that his strength was not sufficient to finish the task, the biker's blood-slimed hands swung down – uselessly, lifelessly and his body sagged, pulling Greer off balance as it slumped to the pavement. There was a gurgling from the severed windpipe, as air bubbled through blood and Greer pulled the garrotte free, wiping it on the biker's t-shirt and thrusting it back into his pocket.

He leaned against the wall, hungrily sucking in the crisp air and exhaling clouds of misty vapour until the terror and the trembling subsided. Sweat-soaked, bloodstained clothes clung to his body like determined cling film, making him shiver, as the frosty night air stole the heat from the moisture. No one had ever fought back like that – the others had accepted their fate, surrendering their pieces of puzzle with hardly any effort at all on his part. *Victims* in every sense of the word.

It was the first time he'd used the garrotte and it would definitely be the last. He had varied his methods of killing in an attempt to hide the fact that the sporadic attacks, which took place in different towns and cities, had anything in common. He covered his tracks by disposing of the bodies in a variety of ways – a few had been found but most would never be discovered – he was sure of that.

A rat scuttled along the gutter, jerking Greer back to his senses. There was still so much to do – the puzzle piece to find, the body to take care of and his own blood-spattered clothes to be disposed of before he returned home. It wasn't until he knelt down next to the body with his filleting knife, that he registered the pain in his thigh…

He turned the tissue-thin segment over in his hand, shaking his head slightly as he remembered the desperate fight for its possession, aware that it had almost cost him his life. Perhaps he was getting too old – for both the killing and the problem-solving. Maybe it was time to quit the Game and give someone younger a chance. The Game Master seemed to be setting ever bigger, ever more intricate riddles but surely that was inevitable? As soon as Greer had completed a Game, the Game Master would have to plan another – more elaborate and more sophisticated than the last. It was a never-ending circle – unless Greer chose to resign, of course.

But gaming was his life – the thrill of the hunt, the pride in his skill at preparing the pieces and finally, the triumphant knowledge that he had beaten the Game Master's challenge – how could he just walk away from that?

And yet...

One day, he would fail to finish the Game.

Who would take up the challenge then?

But he was forgetting that the Game Master was growing older too, was he feeling the pressure of having to be constantly one step ahead of Greer? Perhaps even now, he was coaching his own successor.

It was pointless speculating – this wasn't a club, there was no newsletter to keep him up to date – just the messages in the puzzle fragments to point him in the right direction and move him from place to place, never looking back.

Suddenly, a slow smile of satisfaction crept across his hawkish face as he spotted the link between two of the pieces. He placed the snake-entwined dagger next to the Celtic pattern overlaid with a rosebud. Briefly, memories of finding the pieces flashed through his mind. The snake tattoo had been stripped from the shoulder of a large ginger-haired man, with skin so milky-white that even now, after having been cleaned and dried, it seemed much paler than any of the other pieces. The rosebud had come from the thigh of a girl, whose huge, tear-filled eyes and pleas for mercy had almost touched Greer... but not sufficiently to prevent him silencing her and slicing away the flesh. He had been shocked at his own weakness – true, she was young and the huge eyes in the heart-shaped face framed with chestnut curls gave her a doll-like appeal but he could not afford to be sentimental.

Perhaps it really was time to think about quitting the Game.

He slammed his fists on to the scarred tabletop in frustration, scattering the delicate bits of skin like autumn leaves in a breath of wind.

Shut up! Stop doubting! You just need a rest, that's all.

This had been the most exacting Game so far and it was natural that he would feel tired.

Drained would be a better word, he thought sardonically.

Concentrate.

Once the puzzle had been solved, he could rest before he moved on.

So, concentrate.

Yes! He'd spotted another two pieces that fit together.

He gently picked up the dragon, admiring the beautifully executed artwork and placed it by the Chinese characters. Somewhere on each of these exquisite designs, the Game Maker had inserted his own signature and a clue. Greer doubted that any of the proud owners of the tattoos had ever suspected that their design was anything other than the superficial body adornment that they had requested in the tattoo parlour. Neither would they have guessed that in succumbing to the Game Master's needle, they were signing up to become part of the Game.

Body and Soul.

The chipped coffee mug had been filled, refilled and emptied more times than Greer would ever be able to recall before he finally solved the elaborate puzzle. He gently swept the crumbs from the tabletop, careful not to disturb the final arrangement of tattoos, his many scribbled notes or the map. He must have eaten at some point but he had no recollection of what or when.

It was over.

He leaned back with his hands clasped behind his head, scowling at the tabletop. Usually, he would feel elation despite the gritty eyes and the aching shoulders but this time, the subtle changes in the pieces had disturbed him.

The next Game would begin much further north – there were sufficient clues to guide him to the first tattoo as usual but the pieces had hinted at a new beginning. There had been evidence of two hands wielding the needles in the last two parts of the puzzle and the signature had changed – nothing significant to the untrained eye but Greer had detected the difference and the foreboding chased away any thoughts of triumph.

There was no room for sentiment in the Game but Greer could have sworn there was a suspicion of emotion in the messages of the puzzle. He had the distinct impression the Game Master was signing off and had appointed a successor although it was becoming harder to think straight, now the adrenalin had stopped pumping.

Sleep. I'll think about it when I wake up.

He dreamed of earlier times when he would complete a Game and then go out to celebrate – sleep the last thing on his mind.

When he awoke, he was aware of a strange unsettling feeling, as if something had finished, rather than as if something new was beginning.

It was just the thought of change. Surely, this new Game Master would inject some new blood into the Game – create new challenges, increase the excitement.

But try as he might, Greer could not control the feelings of melancholy, which drew at his guts in a forbidding, yet shapeless way, undermining what would normally have been a triumphant day.

He hastily threw his meagre possessions into a

25

rucksack, taking care only with the collection of tattooed puzzle pieces which he kept in a leather pouch attached to his belt.

He closed the front door of the flat without a backward glance, leaving the impassive table the bearer of a dirty mug, a carton of curdled milk, sufficient money for the rent and the front door key. There would be no irate landlord alerting authorities in his wake. The risks of the Game were great enough without deliberately drawing attention to himself and Greer had worked hard to maintain an anonymous life style – nothing about him was remarkable – he was Mr. Average.

The morning was steely grey, with a cutting wind that did nothing to alleviate Greer's depressed mood. There were few people on the streets and those who were braving the chill walked with their collars up and their heads down, with hands pushed deeply into pockets seeking warmth.

Little chance then, of anyone noticing Greer, which was the only thing that had given him any satisfaction so far today.

The icy air cleared his head and a plan began to form. He would attempt the new puzzle and if it wasn't to his taste, he'd find some way of selling his collection to a would-be gamer, buy a small place, miles from anywhere and settle down.

Not to his taste.

Yes, that was a good way of expressing the never-to-be admitted fear of failure. It didn't matter that he had no idea how he would be able to sell the priceless collection, what was important was that he had a plan. There were always ways and means…

'Got the time, mate?'

Greer swung round in surprise at the youth lurking in the shadow of a disused doorway, and shaking his head, he

26

hurried on, anxious to cut short any conversation.

'Oy! I only asked for the bleedin' time. I ain't after yer money,' sneered the youth. Greer spun round and grabbed the boy by the hoodie, twisting it in his fist and almost lifting the boy off his feet. He was about to throw him back against the wall and walk off when he felt a blow to the back of his head. A sharp, shooting pain spread across his skull and down one shoulder and in his confusion he dropped the boy, staggering on legs that were suddenly unable to support his weight. Another blow to the side of his head felled him completely.

'That's enough! You don't wanna kill him!' said the boy.

'Who cares? He won't be missed. Come on, turn 'im over,' said another voice.

A foot roughly pushed Greer on to his back and as he fought to remain conscious, he felt eager hands scrabbling to untie his belt, pulling at the pouch – faces shrouded by hoodie tops hovering over him slipping in and out of focus.

'Got 'em?'

'Yeah! Here they are. We're in the Game! No one'll stop us now!'

'What we gonna do with 'im?'

'Has 'e got any tatts? We could always practise on 'im.'

'Don't matter if 'e does or not, we can still practise.'

'Yeah, s'pose.'

The new Game had begun...

A Hell Of A Time

Death had come suddenly.

One moment I'd been stretching to reach the top corner of the window pane with a cloth and the next, I was cart wheeling through the air as I plummeted to earth. I don't suppose it took more than a few seconds to fall from the top of the ladder to the patio, yet I had time to see the bucket spill its soapy contents over Beryl, who was steadying the foot of the ladder and to hear her yell as she dived sideways out of the way.

My high-pitched scream chased me downwards through the air. It was the last sound that I heard. Thankfully, I was spared whatever sickening noise my body made as it hit the paving stones.

And that was it.

I, Matthew Norris, was no more.

Now, I've never had much time for religion.

You know how it is.

Making a living is a full time job and once you acquire a wife, two children and a mortgage, there's no time to sit and contemplate your navel.

There are car repayments, insurance, three weeks holiday in Florida to be paid for and so on and so on. Arguably, if money hadn't been so tight, I wouldn't have been cleaning the windows against Beryl's wishes. She'd begged me to get a window cleaner. But why pay someone to do something you can do yourself?

But forget life. Here I was, dead.

So, what of death?

Of course, even I, with my lack of religious knowledge, knew about Heaven and Hell but rather than blue skies and fluffy clouds, or fire and brimstone, I found myself surrounded by a thick impenetrable fog.

Perhaps this was it.

Perhaps I was going to spend the rest of my life... well, death – waiting inside a cloud.

I began to panic. This couldn't be it, surely? To have such an untimely end after all that earthly struggle, and then to be abandoned for eternity. What an anticlimax.

I strained to see – something – anything – through the obscurity and gradually, I realised with relief that the mist was beginning to lift.

I was in an enormous, bare hall – about the size of an aircraft hangar – and ahead of me, sat a figure at a desk. Behind him were two unmarked doors.

He put down his nail file and rifled through some papers.

'Matthew Norris?' he called in a thin, reedy voice.

'That's me,' I replied stepping forward.

'Sign here and here,' he said in the voice of someone who had much more important things to do, and once I'd signed, he put the paper in a drawer. 'Take the left hand door,' he said, jerking his thumb over his shoulder and sliding a folder towards me 'Hand this in at reception.' He picked up his file again and inspected his nails.

'Er, I wonder if you could fill me in a bit on the arrangements. I'm new here and I'm not sure what...'

'Left hand door,' he said, pointing with his beautifully manicured finger.

'But I was just wondering,' I persisted, 'about Heaven and Hell... I mean, some people say they don't exist. So, I was just wondering... are they real?'

'Of course,' he said looking at me as if I was an imbecile. 'Now, move along please. Left hand door.'

'Just one more thing,' I said ignoring his look of annoyance, 'where does the left hand door lead?'

He snorted. 'Well, I'll give you a clue. It begins with H and E.'

I snatched my folder and headed for the door.

'And ends in L and L,' I heard him mutter under his breath.

I made for the right hand door.

'Don't even think about it, Buster,' he said without looking round.

On the other side of the left hand door, I was surprised to find myself in a large, airy room. Neutral colours and tasteful pictures on the walls.

No fire or brimstone. No gnashing of teeth.

I handed my folder in at reception where I was given an information booklet and told to join the long queue.

'This ain't so bad,' remarked the old man in front of me, 'I was expecting something much worse than this. Look,' he said stabbing at his booklet with a gnarled finger, 'it's even got a swimming pool. See, here are the opening times. Pity I'm afraid of water. Yeah, great pity. Wouldn't have drowned if I'd learned to swim.'

I looked at my folder booklet expecting to see the same information. But mine was different. Where the old man had swimming pool opening times, I had information about the climbing wall. That would be something that I definitely wouldn't be taking advantage of – after my fall from the top of the ladder, the thought of heights made my head swim. The rest of the booklet contained a short welcome message, opening times of the restaurant, a few rules etc. etc.

Perhaps they were trying to lull us into a false sense of security. Whoever 'they' were.

Eventually, I reached the head of the queue where I was handed another folder by a young man who didn't make eye contact. He directed me to yet another door and in a monotone, instructed me to make myself at home.

'Excuse me,' I said 'but this isn't quite what I was expecting…'

'Expecting?'

'Well, not exactly expecting but I just thought that Hell was supposed to be... well, painful. This all looks very comfortable... not that I'm complaining or anything but haven't you rather misrepresented yourselves on Earth? There are some people up there who try really hard to lead good lives. Why should they bother when Hell is... so comfortable.'

'Life... and Hell are of your own making. What you do with your time here is up to you.' He gestured to me to move on and held out a folder to the woman behind me.

I had nothing to lose, so I persisted, 'Well, it just seems to me—'

'Look! I'm not interested in how it seems to you. You no longer have a say in what goes on. You do, however, have two choices. You can read the contents of your folder. Or not. I'll check with you in a few millennia to see how 'comfortable' you're still finding things.'

Smart Alec, I thought as I opened the door.

I was in another large hall filled with leather sofas and chairs, coffee tables and pot plants. Many of the chairs were occupied but strangely, no one spoke. Some people were reading the contents of their folders, others were staring into space, a few paced back and forth – everyone seemed to be deep in thought and by the frowns and sighs, their thoughts weren't bringing them much joy.

I sat down and looked at my folder.

'Open with Caution' it said on the cover.

I hesitated. Perhaps I wouldn't open it at all.

'You'll open it in the end,' whispered a woman as she walked past me, 'we all do. You won't be able to last for eternity wondering what's inside.'

I opened it.

There was one single sheet of paper.

31

On it was a list of all the occasions when a different action or decision would have resulted in my life taking a different direction.

...The night you told your best friend that his girl, Beryl, was cheating, so he would finish with her and you could ask her out, you missed a phone call from Marcia Bentley. Had you taken that call, you would have married Marcia, instead of Beryl...

Marcia Bentley! Beautiful, intelligent and more importantly, rich Marcia Bentley. And she had been interested in me!

I sagged into the plush leather chair, my mind whirring with the implications.

...The day you let your boss win at golf was the day that he decided to promote Bill Marshall instead of you. He values honesty not false flattery...

Promotion to area manager had been *that* close! And slimy Bill Marshall had got the job because I'd let the boss win at golf. This was unbelievable.

I read on discovering all the twists and turns of my life where the outcome could have been so different – so much better. If only I'd known, my life would have been perfect.

I placed my head in my hands and moaned gently. I couldn't bear to read any more.

The sheet slipped onto the floor

'…If you hadn't run up such a credit card bill and hadn't dismissed the window cleaner, you wouldn't have lost your balance and fallen off the ladder…,' the man next to me read out loud, as he handed the sheet back, 'Shame,' he said without emotion. I snatched the paper from him. It was bad enough that I faced the prospect of spending eternity knowing how my life could have turned out if I had just done this or just done that, without everyone else knowing.

I sank into the leather armchair and held my head in my

hands. So, I thought, Hell wasn't a place of oppressive heat and torture by pitchfork. It was a state of mind – of perpetual regret at past misconduct and missed opportunities. I thrust the paper into my pocket angrily. I would forget… I would clear my mind, erase the memories or I would surely go mad…

Leave It To Lester

Lester fidgeted on the uncomfortable, straight-backed chair in the doctor's waiting room. He was surrounded by patients waiting for their treatment, all of whom, like him, had shaven heads with a tattooed ring encircling each scalp – the marks of a Servile.

Each Servile stared silently ahead, not making eye contact. It was forbidden to fraternise and no one dared disobey.

What was there to say, anyway? They were there simply to have their three-monthly inoculations – or so they thought.

Prior to the many 'inoculations' Lester had received, he'd believed the story too – but now, he wasn't sure what he was about to be given – although he had a rough idea of what was about to be taken from him.

He'd overheard his master on the phone to Dr Bentley yesterday pleading for an appointment.

'Yes, I know he's overdue, that's why I need him done as soon as possible.'

Lester had been about to enter the study to remove the breakfast dishes when he realised Master was referring to him. He stopped and pressed his ear to the door, feeling guilty about listening although not knowing why. Usually guilt followed a reprimand from Master – an angry word if he spilled tea in the saucer, a curse if he couldn't find exactly what he'd been asked to buy in the market and sometimes a blow if he hadn't served dinner and gone to his room before Master's latest girl arrived. And then Lester would feel guilty because he obviously hadn't given good service.

But this time, he'd recognised he'd done something wrong himself and the recognition had given rise to guilt.

How strange!

Of course, he'd never actually been told not to listen to Master's conversations but then before today, he'd never taken an interest in anything that didn't concern him.

But apparently this *did* concern him.

It was all very puzzling.

'Yes, I know it's not advisable to leave it more than three months. I've been really busy lately and I forgot to book him in.' Master drummed his fingers on the desk indicating his displeasure at not having his wishes carried out immediately – a sign Lester recognised and tried hard to avoid.

'No, it won't happen again but he needs the brain wipe and insertion now. Can you fit him in?' Master's voice began to rise as he became more irritated.

'Well, no, I haven't noticed anything specifically wrong but he's not as servile as usual and his free thinking is coming back... A stronger dose? You can do that? How much?... *How much?* That's twice the normal price!... Yeah, yeah. Well, if it keeps him servile for longer, I guess it's gotta be worth it. I'll send him along tomorrow, thanks for fitting him in...'

Lester stumbled back to the kitchen. He knew he'd encounter the tapping fingers when he finally collected the breakfast dishes but before he could look Master in the eyes, he needed to think.

No easy task, as his thoughts, which normally seemed well ordered and predictable, were now buzzing round his head like moths round a flame, crashing and burning in panic.

Brain Wipe and *Insertion*.

Well, *Brain Wipe* sounded self-explanatory.

But *Insertion*. Insertion of what?

Lester had no idea but he was sure it wasn't the injection

all the other expressionless Serviles sitting in the doctor's waiting room assumed they were getting.

The overheard telephone conversation had shaken the foundations of his world. For the first time, he felt vulnerable and afraid and the worst thing was, he had no idea why. Master looked after him, providing a room, food and everything he needed. He was indeed master of Lester's life. So if Lester was being sent for a jab or whatever it was, it was surely for his benefit.

Wasn't it?

But the telephone conversation had been deeply unsettling and besides that, for the last week or so, strange thoughts had been creeping into his consciousness and disturbing him.

Thoughts of *fairness*, of *independence*, of *freedom*.

Lester wasn't even sure he could define *fairness*, *independence* and *freedom* but he'd suddenly become aware of the lack of them. Whereas it had once been his life's ambition to server Master in return for protection and a home, he was beginning to see how much work he did for a lazy, dictatorial man in exchange for a tiny, cold room and scraps of food.

'Leave it to Lester, Sir,' he'd proudly say when Master demanded something.

Why hadn't he noticed the inequality in the relationship before?

Why had he never experienced dissatisfaction before?

Before?

Before what? Before when?

Instinctively he felt his whole life had been spent serving Master, but trying to remember past the last few days was like staring into the blackest night looking for a crow.

He needed information and he needed it fast but until

today, everything he required to carry out his duties was already there in his brain.

Although the prospect of *Brain Wipe* was alarming, Lester was even more terrified by the thought of *Insertion*. The former implied something being removed – and that was bad enough, but the latter suggested the introduction of something into his brain that shouldn't be there.

He'd been making his bed that morning, when he remembered there was a journal hidden under the mattress. He'd pulled it out and turned it over carefully in his hand. It felt like he'd never laid eyes on it before but the entries were in his hand writing. The last time he'd written anything had been three months ago and then again, just over three months before that. In between those entries, there was nothing at all in the book and nothing stored in his memory. He carefully recorded the overheard conversation in the journal so that in three months' time, he might stumble across it and warn himself that for a brief period of time he'd be able to think and wonder, before his memory and reason were stolen and replaced with – well, who knew what? Presumably, if his master's comments were anything to go by, something that ensured he carried out the duties of a servant with such dedication and devotion, there was room for no independent thought.

Something that ensured his master could 'Leave it all to Lester'.

Dr Bentley shepherded one of the Serviles out of his surgery. 'Sit down till you feel better, Mason. Nurse'll phone your master and say you'll be later than expected.'

Mason gripped the sides of the waiting room chair; face grey, eyes staring into the distance and breath coming in staccato gasps. All the other Serviles had walked calmly from the surgery, with vacant, lifeless expressions and

Lester wondered what was wrong with him.

By the time the two Serviles ahead of Lester had emerged from the surgery, Mason's breathing had quietened and other than twitching spasmodically, his hands now lay motionless in his lap. With glazed, unblinking eyes, he looked at the wall.

Lester fought the urge to run away, as he was summoned into the doctor's room. But there was nowhere to go and no hope of outwitting the system.

He might as well go in and get it over with.

'Lester!' the nurse said sharply, 'Don't keep Doctor waiting.'

'Lie down and tilt your head back,' Dr Bentley ordered, without looking up as Lester hovered in the doorway. Removing something with forceps from a Petri dish, he placed it on a tray and viewed it through a large illuminated, magnifying glass.

From his position on the couch, Lester could see him inject something into the small, white object.

'What exactly are you going to give me?' asked Lester. He didn't expect an answer but it was worth a shot.

'Since you've asked the question, Lester, it's obvious your last brain wipe's worn off. I'm going to carry out a little procedure. It'll take away your free thinking and install all the information you need to serve your master. But you won't remember anything I tell you, so don't worry about it. Now, just relax, you're going to have to be patient, I'm afraid. I've had to use a larger carrier than I would normally because your master wants you to have a higher dose than usual. It'll take slightly longer to penetrate but once it's in place, you won't remember the sensation at all.'

The doctor clamped Lester's jaw with a rubber-gloved hand, pinning his face to the couch and with the other, he brought the small, white object held delicately with forceps, towards Lester's face.

If he hadn't been held so rigidly, Lester would have screamed.

'You've got your master to thank for this, I'm afraid. If he spent more time organising his life and less romping in bed, he'd send you before your free thinking returned, then you wouldn't know what was going on and this wouldn't seem so distasteful. But trust me, once the Tunneller Worm's burrowed into your brain, it'll die and decompose quite rapidly, delivering the implant in a reasonably pain-free way. Don't fight me, there's a good chap. The couch has restricting bands, which I'll use if you don't hold still, so this is going up your nose, one way or the other.'

Lester let go of the rubber-gloved hand that was nearly breaking his jaw and tried to relax. There was no point fighting. He squeezed his eyes shut, to block the sight of the tiny, pulsating worm and tried to hold the memory of the journal in the centre of his mind but with a higher dose, he'd be lucky to find it in three months.

He'd be lucky if he ever found it again.

Once released from the grip of the forceps, the worm squirmed round Lester's nostril, wriggling higher and higher.

Lester held his breath.

Inhaling would surely speed the worm on its journey up to the bone and tissues that separated nose from brain.

The sound of chairs scraping, a thud and a scream reverberated through the room.

'Doctor!' the nurse shouted.

'Stay there!' Dr Bentley released his hold on Lester's face and ran for the door.

'Well, pick him up, Nurse! He's passed out – not died! Take him in the side room. I'll be in to see him in a second.

Look, he's already coming round…Mason? Mason? There's a good chap. Now go with Nurse. She'll take you to lie down.'

Lester wasted no time. He held his fingers to the top of his nose and squeezed hard. If he were too late, he'd speed the worm upwards but if not…

He released his grip and snorted. Creamy liquid dribbled out of his nostril, which he quickly wiped away with his sleeve and laid immobile as Dr Bentley came back. Making an enormous effort to relax, he stared blankly into the distance and hoped no more fluid from the squashed worm would trickle out of his nose.

'Feeling okay?' Dr Bentley asked.

Lester nodded. He had no idea what he should say or how he should behave but recalling Mason's vacant expression, he assumed that whatever he did, should be done with complete lack of animation.

'Hmm,' the doctor didn't sound convinced but before he could ask any questions, the phone rang and as he answered, he dismissed Lester with a wave of his hand.

More viscous fluid drained from Lester's nostril and he wiped it away quickly, wincing as something small and sharp scraped his top lip. He pinched the minute object between forefinger and thumb and made his escape.

As soon as he was out of sight of the surgery, he looked at the tiny dot, which was now pressed into the pad of his thumb. It was a tiny, metallic capsule, still coated in white material from the squashed Tunneller Worm – the implant containing all the information necessary to make him an able and willing servant.

Lester flicked it into a nearby hedge.

Now what?

As soon as it was obvious the brain wipe and insertion hadn't worked, Lester would be sent back to Dr Bentley.

Unless, of course, he could keep up the pretence of servility. But he wasn't prepared for the shady world of charades that opened up before him. Life had once been so simple. How long would he be able to keep it up? And even if he could convince Master he was servile, in another three months' time, he'd be sent back to Dr Bentley's again.

There was no other choice – he had to escape.

But *escape* was just a word. Exactly what it entailed, Lester had no idea. He knew nothing about the world outside Master's house and there was no one to ask. For as long as he could remember, life had simply involved serving. There had been no time to learn anything new and no need. Everything he was required to know was right there in his brain – how Master liked his eggs cooked in the morning, how he liked his underwear arranged in the drawer but there was nothing in Lester's head that would help him now.

I have to think like a master, he thought and was so astonished that such a notion had popped into his mind, he stopped abruptly, causing a minor incident when the Servile behind almost ran into him with a baby buggy.

Lester muttered an apology and hurried off, eyes downcast.

This was not going to be easy.

He was only allowed to touch Master's books to dust them and he'd been expressly forbidden to go anywhere near the Internet tablet, which was usually locked in the desk drawer. But he was going to have to gain access to information somehow – even if it was an enormous risk – and in the meantime, he'd have to maintain a veneer of servility and hope his master was too preoccupied with the latest girl to notice.

On the way home, Lester realised he'd had an idea. It pleased him greatly.

He couldn't remember ever having had an idea before and the cleverness of its conception and form amazed and alarmed him in equal measure.

He knocked on Master's study door and entered.

'Dr Bentley said I may not be myself for a day or two after the inoculation, Sir,' he said, careful to keep his eyes vacant and to speak in a toneless voice – despite his breath coming in short, sharp bursts.

'But you feel all right?'

'Oh yes, Sir,'

'Good because I've got a friend coming over this evening and it'll be rather inconvenient if you aren't well.'

'Just leave it to Lester as normal, Sir. I'm well – it's just that I may not behave as I usually do.' It was just as well to emphasize the lie in case Master hadn't taken it in the first time.

Lester's heart was thumping so hard, he crossed his arms over his chest, worried it might actually burst through his ribs.

But Master had already turned away.

'My friend's coming at seven o'clock,' he called over his shoulder as he ran upstairs, 'I'll open the door. All I want you to do, is make sure dinner's on the table at half past seven. Go and tidy my bedroom now, then keep out of sight till morning.'

'Yes, Sir, leave it to Lester.'

Perhaps it would be easier to get hold of the Internet tablet than he'd thought. At one time, when he'd been told to keep out of sight, he'd have gone straight to his room and … and what? Gone to bed? Stared at the wall? He didn't know.

But now he'd have access to the Internet all night.

42

He knew Master's latest girl had arrived when her raucous, braying laugh floated down to his room. He was tempted to creep upstairs to find out what the owner of such an ugly sound looked like but he had more important things to do. He'd only ever been within walking distance from Master's house with nothing more on his mind than finding the best bargains in the market.

How would he survive in the real world?

Who could he trust?

How far would he have to walk before there were no more houses?

Or did the city go on for ever?

Questions, questions. It was really all quite daunting.

Lester flitted from website to website, soaking up information but it was mainly relevant to masters and useless for planning an escape.

Information *for* masters *by* masters.

That wasn't surprising of course, but it was hard to put together a rational overview of the world.

And then he stumbled across the first hint there were others out there who weren't locked in the Master-Servile relationship. Somehow a small group of people had placed a message on the Internet – a series of short video clips, put together in such a disjointed way it was hard to make any sense of them but it seemed each of individuals was looking for something – just like Lester. They were led by an attractive red-haired girl but the others looked like no one he'd ever encountered. Lester guessed one of them was a robot, another was like a man but his face was disfigured and he obviously had some sort of paralysis as he staggered rather than walked. Lester wasn't sure the fourth person was a person at all. It was hairy and had whiskers like an animal but it spoke and stood on its back legs like a man. Each clip lasted for a second or two, giving Lester a tantalising glimpse of a colourful world that was unlike anything he'd ever seen.

He was mesmerised.

What did it mean?

He didn't know but he was determined to find out.

The original plan had been to wait a day or two until he'd gained some more knowledge but now he knew there were other people out there on a quest, he was eager to find them.

He jumped as the phone buzzed.

'Lester, we've run out of champagne. Bring up some more.' Master slammed down the phone.

Lester groaned – he'd made a major mistake in forgetting to stock up the fridge in Master's bedroom.

How many more had he made?

And how much longer before Master discovered there had been no 'inoculation' and sent him back to Dr Bentley?

It was all very well knowing there were like-minded people out there but Lester needed more time to research the girl, her strange friends and how to find them.

But he might be out of time as soon as the loud girl left. Unless…

Unless he prolonged her stay. After a brief search in the medicine cabinet, he found the sleeping tablets Master often took when he didn't have company and popped them all out of the blister pack into the palm of his hand. Dropping them in the champagne, he swirled the bottle gently and forced the cork back in place.

Would they dissolve?

He dared not delay any longer while he watched them disappear, so he jiggled the tray as he walked, trying to agitate the bottle while keeping the glasses in place. When he arrived upstairs, he placed the tray on the floor and shook the bottle one last time. He rapped three times on the door and rushed for the stairs before Master had time to open it. The sound of the door opening and closing, followed by clinking glasses and laughter, followed Lester as he raced down the stairs.

'Whoa!' shouted Master, as the cork hit the ceiling with force, and there was the sound of liquid splashing in a glass. The girl roared with delight.

Downstairs in the entrance hall, Lester cursed himself for shaking the bottle so vigorously and wondered if an undissolved tablet might have bubbled out of the bottle. And if it hadn't, would they be able to detect the taste?

The jarring laughter continued, and Lester crept back upstairs, straining to hear. As the minutes passed, the giggling grew quieter until it stopped. Suddenly, the door flew open and Master shouted 'Leshter, get an ambulansh. My friend'sh been taken ill. Leshter? Lesh...' He slid gently to the floor, where he lay, motionless.

It hadn't occurred to Lester that Master and the girl would do anything other than fall asleep and wake up hours later believing they'd drunk too much. But perhaps the tablets really had made them ill.

Or worse – perhaps he'd killed them.

For the first time, Lester began to wonder if he wouldn't have been better off if the brain wipe and insertion had taken place but it was too late. Fear, panic and a longing for freedom jostled for place in his brain.

He had no choice; he had to leave now and try to find the red-haired girl and her friends. But suppose he couldn't find them? Or worse, suppose they wouldn't let him join them?

Then Lester had another idea.

They wouldn't be able to refuse if he took gifts – and he knew where he could get the very things that two of the group were seeking.

Surely they'd accept him then!

Lester ran down to the basement and threw a few tools into a bag. He'd seen Master use them occasionally although he'd never taken much interest and he hoped they weren't too complicated. Taking the stairs two at time, his heart hammering in his chest, he reached Master's bedroom. He plugged in the circular saw and stood over the girl, who was spread-eagled on the floor next to the bed. She was naked, her blonde hair fanned out as if she'd collapsed backwards and Lester wondered how such an ugly laugh could emanate from such an innocent, sweet-looking girl. She sighed, shivering slightly and Lester pulled the bedcover over her nakedness.

Closing the front door for the last time, Lester clutched the rucksack tightly and pulled the hood of Master's jacket forward to hide his face. Any covering which hid a Servile's shaven, tattooed head was forbidden and if he was recognised, he'd soon be escorted home or taken to the police station. Thankfully, he only passed two masters as he took the familiar route towards the marketplace and both of them walked quickly, heads down and collars up against the driving rain as they picked their way between the puddles. On reflection, it would have been sensible to bring a warm coat but there was no going back now, just a few more streets and he'd be in uncharted territory and then there'd be no danger of anyone recognising him. If he kept walking, he might reach the edge of the city before first light – if indeed there was an edge. But the city must end somewhere, surely? If he didn't find it before morning, perhaps he'd come across somewhere to hide until darkness fell again.

Lester couldn't tell if it was fear or excitement that was making his pulse race.

Perhaps it was both.

I will succeed because I am courageous, he thought, pleased because he liked the idea of being courageous and also because until yesterday while he was searching the Internet, he hadn't known what *courage* was and now he could actually claim to have some. But there was obviously more to learn about courage than the simple definition he'd stumbled across, because as far as he could see, it was something you generated yourself, not something you could find. And yet, the red-haired girl's friend – the one who looked like an animal – was searching for that very thing. Well, Lester would keep an eye out on his journey although he doubted he'd find any. He looked down at the rucksack clutched tightly to his chest and noticed dark drops were leaking from the bottom and splashing into the puddles on the ground.

More blood!

It was hard to believe a body could hold so much, especially Master's.

Cutting out the braying girl's brain hadn't resulted in as much blood as Master's heart. The red, pulsing fountain that erupted from Master's chest as he cut into the flesh had been completely unexpected as it momentarily blinded him.

His courage had nearly failed when Master opened his eyes just as the circular saw bit into his chest. For a second, the instinct to obey took over and if Master had been able to speak, Lester would have stopped, ready to carry out any orders but the sounds that came out of Master's mouth were as incomprehensible as the piteous, silent appeal in his eyes. Lester was used to commands and reprimands – he had no experience of being asked to do something, especially if the request was silent and seen only in the eyes of a dying man.

Well, it didn't matter now. Lester was free and there

47

would be no more demands and orders for him!

The blood would soon wash away in the rain, just as it had in the shower after all that nasty, messy sawing, and Lester would never think about Master – or his orders again – except possibly when he handed over his precious gifts.

Leave it to Lester, he thought with satisfaction.

The heart for the robot.

The brain for the staggering man.

And when he found some, – courage for the animal-man.

It shouldn't be too difficult to find the red-haired girl and her friends once he'd found the edge of the city. He knew which road they were following and a yellow brick road couldn't be that hard to find.

To Sleep – Perchance To Live

Roscoe had been throwing up in the latrine when the shuttle docked with Station Genesis III.

If Sergeant Driscoll had followed Scientific Exploration of Space guidelines, which stated that all passengers should be strapped in their seats during landing and docking, Roscoe would be dead – his body riddled with bullets and his blood mingling and coalescing with that of the other soldiers and crew.

In fact, if Roscoe hadn't been kneeling over the bowl, retching, the bullets that penetrated the door at what would have been chest height, would now be buried deep in his body and he would have died alone – yards from his comrades, locked in the stinking cramped room.

But luck had been with him.

Or had it?

What was he going to do now? Perhaps he'd be better off dead than alone on a scientific station so far from home. For all he knew, he and the homicidal maniac might be the only people on Genesis III.

The shuttle and its crew had been sent to investigate a malfunction in the communication system and to deliver special drugs, so there had obviously been some sort of problem in this lonely outpost, whirling in space.

He crouched with his ear to the door. Thankfully, the surge of adrenalin must have pulled rank over whatever was causing the nausea, and his sickness had ceased.

What was going on out there?

Had any of the crew survived?

It seemed unlikely, as the last time he'd seen them, they'd all been unarmed and strapped in; the weapons safely stored in the hold.

Had the attacker spotted the empty seat and realised

49

there was someone else on board? He searched desperately for some means of escape but the latrine was more of a cupboard – small and bare – other than the toilet and sink.

Through the door, he could hear grunts and muffled sounds, which suddenly gave way to a scream so piercing and inhuman, Roscoe threw himself backwards against the toilet bowl, his hands over his mouth to stop him from joining in.

What sort of creature was out there?

A single gunshot rang out, turning the scream to a sickening gurgle. There was a soft thud, the clatter of metal against metal, as something about the weight of a gun, hit the floor and then silence.

Roscoe crouched down again, ear against the door, straining for any sound to tell him what was happening.

Had the killer shot himself? What if there were several of them out there?

Should he risk opening the door?

The Scientific Exploration of Space military training had been rigorous but in a universe where there'd been no serious conflict for the past 20 years, such an eventuality had never been addressed.

For the first time ever, Roscoe longed for the peace of his father's farm, even the rhythmic routine that had once bored him stupid. Perhaps if he'd been more proactive, the farm might have prospered...

Perhaps if he'd even taken an interest...

But he'd longed for action or at least a change. When SES had started recruiting, he'd been more than happy to sign up.

A scientific station orbiting Earth, from whom no communication had been received for several weeks, and a few scientists who needed special drugs hadn't sounded like a risky undertaking. There'd been whispers of alien invasion but no one with any sense had taken them seriously.

All sorts of possibilities now ran riot through Roscoe's imagination, as he mentally replayed conversations between those of the crew who'd seen far more of the universe than he could dream of.

And now, those people's lives had been cut tragically short while on what should have been a routine mission.

The loss of contact between Genesis III and SES was possibly due to computer failure and as the nature of the problem was unknown, the shuttle carried sufficient parts to construct everything necessary to restore communications. It was highly unusual for a communication system to simply stop, considering the inbuilt features which prevented failure. In the unlikely event of total malfunction, error messages would normally be generated and received on Earth to allow a rescue mission to be sent with the correct personnel and computer parts as speedily as possible.

Genesis III had simply gone silent.

It was all very strange – but no machine was infallible.

The station was manned by scientists carrying out studies and developing new ways for self-contained stations to be established across the universe. Eventually small pockets of humanity would relocate to such stations, relieving the over-populated and under-resourced Earth.

It should have been such an easy assignment...

Footsteps and shouts set Roscoe's heart beating like a buffalo stampede.

'What the...?' a male voice boomed out giving Roscoe a glimmer of hope.

Whoever had spoken was obviously shocked – not the reaction of a gun-toting madman.

'I'll call Dr Collier,' said another voice, this time

female, 'someone may have survived.'

Others joined the man and woman, and voices rose in pitch and volume as people reacted to the scene that Roscoe could only imagine, and whose brain was struggling to block.

It was time to open the door.

There was a shocked silence as he emerged.

He was a startling sight; eyes wide in horror as he surveyed what remained of his comrades and dried vomit on his chin.

'Get him!' ordered the man who'd been first on the scene.

Before Roscoe could react, two men had grabbed him, pinning his arms behind his back.

'Mason, for goodness sake!' said the woman, 'He's no threat! Look at him, he's as shocked as we are!'

'Under the current situation, Jenner, he's a suspect. We don't know what happened here and we don't know him...'

'Yyyou surely don't think I did this?' stammered Roscoe.

'Sedate him,' ordered Mason. 'We'll deal with him later when we've cleared up this mess.'

One of the men held something to the struggling Roscoe's temple. Fireworks went off in his head and within seconds, he was dangling limply between his captors.

The stark light of the medical unit penetrated Roscoe's eyelids and sliced into his consciousness.

'Collier, I think he's coming round.' It was the voice of the woman who'd objected to him being sedated.

There was a whir and click as something was held next to his neck.

'Blood pressure's returning to normal. He'll live,' said Collier.

'Good. Mason was completely out of line ordering him to be sedated. Who does he think he is? He's the Head of Scientific Studies not a soldier. I'm going to make a full report. Prof. Villiers is going to go mental...'

Jenner broke off abruptly and there was a pause, which even Roscoe with his tenuous grip on consciousness could determine was charged with unease.

'I mean *furious*. Villiers'll be furious... Anyway, as things are so critical at the moment, Villiers has got enough on his mind without Mason going all alpha male.'

'We might need someone who's willing to assume a military role. I'd certainly feel safer with someone like Mason taking charge. Things are getting completely out of control and Villiers isn't doing anything. He seems to have withdrawn completely. He hasn't even visited the shuttle since the shooting. It's like he's given up.' Collier paused. 'A whole envoy of guards wiped out by Brazier! The most gentle man on Genesis III. I just can't believe it!'

'Are we sure it *was* Brazier? P'raps he just got caught in the crossfire...'

'No, it was definitely him. All the crew were strapped in and no one could have got out of the shuttle after the attack without being seen.'

'Why on earth would Brazier have done that?'

'I don't know. I was treating him for severe stress and depression but he didn't seem violent. I just don't understand it...'

'And then to turn the gun on himself... Unbelievable! And after Floriano. I mean, what're the chances of two men becoming so disturbed that they turn violent and then commit suicide? It's not like it's a high pressure environment. We're pretty much left to get on with our own research. So long as a weekly report is filed to Prof. Villiers, no one's on your back. Mason's work is the most high-profile because he's in charge of food production and atmosphere. But Floriano and Brazier! How random is that?'

'It might not be quite as random as you think.'

'What d'you mean?'

'Floriano was the first to complain of the symptoms and then about three months later, Brazier came to see me... and then eight others. Two of those died. It seems to start with insomnia, then symptoms in-keeping with sleep deprivation. Most people who say they're insomniacs sleep more than they realise but Brazier and the others completely lost the ability to sleep. I've never seen anything like it. Sedation didn't work – in fact if anything, they became more agitated.'

'Two people died? When? I didn't know!'

'Villiers wanted it kept quiet.'

'Why?'

'I guess he didn't want anyone to panic.'

'And now you're telling me we've got six more ticking time bombs on this station?'

'Yep. Villier's had them all confined to quarters. The SES party were supposed to bring some experimental drugs and if they didn't work, the patients were going to be quarantined and taken back to Earth.'

'Quarantine? D'you think it's infectious?'

'Hard to say. None of the affected people worked together but the whole station runs off bacteria – food and atmosphere production, waste processing... If something had mutated, it wouldn't be a complete surprise.'

'No, we've been really careful, tests didn't show any hazardous changes in the bacteria. I know there was slight fungal contamination of the food vats a while ago but that was contained and eliminated before anyone could've been affected.'

'So they say...'

'What d'you mean? I did the tests myself. There definitely hasn't been any mutation and Mason detected the fungus before it entered the food chain. The vats were cleaned out and restocked before there was any threat,' said Jenner indignantly.

'Well, I was on a different space station a few years back and they had some sort of contamination of the food supply. It took over a week to get things back on track with all the cleaning and restocking of bacteria. Here it was supposed to have taken a day.'

'P'raps there are faster ways of doing things nowadays.'

'Possibly ...'

There was silence for a few minutes.

Dr Collier periodically held instruments to Roscoe's neck and typed results into a computer tablet.

'You know, it's funny – everything's changed since the food vats were disconnected,' mused Jenner, 'Mason took over my work and sent me around the station doing all sorts of meaningless stuff. I haven't filed any reports for some time but Villiers hasn't mentioned it. It's like Mason just wanted me out of the lab. I mean, why've I got to babysit this soldier? I'm a microbiologist, not a nurse. But now, whenever I ask about my research work, Mason changes the subject. He's so defensive and distracted.' Jenner paused for a second, 'You don't think he's getting the same thing as Floriano, Brazier and the others do you?'

'Who knows? The first sign's insomnia. You can hide that for a while...'

'Well, he's always been moody, so it's hard to know if he's depressed but I guess he's got to provide food and air for the whole station – that's quite a responsibility and if we've got lunatics running round with weapons, casually killing people, it can't make things easy.'

Roscoe groaned and partially opened his eyes.

'He's coming round,' said Collier, 'Have you found out anything about him?'

'Yeah, I've got the information off his chip. His name's Roscoe. Rookie soldier. He joined SES a few months ago.'

Dr Collier held something to Roscoe's temple which radiated a soothing coolness through his brain, calming the skull-splitting hammering.

'Gently, Roscoe,' Jenner said as he tried to gulp down the cool water she held to his lips, 'you don't want to be sick again.'

He savoured the water which slipped satin-smooth across his parched tongue, washing away the taste of stale vomit.

The door opened with a swish and Mason strode in. He scowled at Jenner.

'Isn't he up yet?'

'He wouldn't have been in this state if you hadn't been so heavy-handed,' said Jenner.

'I need to talk to him now. How are you soldier?' said Mason, ignoring her.

'I'm okay, Sir.'

'We urgently need the drugs you bought. Can you get them for me?'

A siren shrieked, halting Dr Collier's objection to taking Roscoe before she considered him ready. The piercing sound faltered slightly and died as the lights dimmed. For a second there was silence. The ever present hum of generators ceased and the only sound in the eerie stillness was Mason's curse. Dr Collier, who was familiar with the layout of the sick bay had already reached the life support pod and removed four emergency packs which she handed out. Each contained a flask of water and a mask with a small bacterial reservoir which would produce sufficient air for three days. Just as they were about to open the kits, the lights and power returned.

'Jenner, take the soldier to the shuttle and find the drugs. I'm going to see what's happening to the power. The back-up generators have kicked in but keep the masks with you just in case.' Mason strode to the door as Jenner muttered under her breath 'Yes, Sir!'

She tucked two masks in her pocket and helped Roscoe to his feet.

'You okay?' she asked as he staggered slightly.

'He's not ready for this,' protested Dr Collier, 'that was a massive dose of sedative they gave him...'

'I'm fine,' said Roscoe, 'let's go.'

The sooner he delivered the drugs and got word to SES HQ, the sooner he'd be on his way back home. Of course, he'd have to wait until a relief shuttle was sent to pick him up. It took a minimum of two people to fly any craft in the fleet. Although there would definitely be someone on board Genesis III who was licensed to fly, he was reluctant to share a confined space in the middle of infinity with a potential killer. From Jenner and Collier's conversation, whatever it was that was affecting these scientists, seemed to be imperceptible until the victim suddenly turned into a homicidal maniac.

Dr Collier had been right. Roscoe wasn't ready – after a few steps, he realised he felt like a puppet whose strings had been replaced with elastic, and putting his hand against the wall, he steadied himself.

Everything was rippling, and ahead of him, two Jenners strode side by side, fading in and out of focus. He squeezed his eyes shut and opened them again, trying to clear his vision. To his relief, when he looked again, the two Jenners began to slide towards each other and merged into one but the rest of his body was lagging behind his eyes in recovering, and there was a delay before his leg muscles responded to orders from his brain. It felt as though he was creeping slowly through what appeared to be an undulating corridor and in this shifting, surreal world, it was easy to imagine something alien had taken hold.

Don't be ridiculous, it's just the sedative. It'll wear off. The problem here is human, not alien. Human, not alien. Human, not...

When Jenner realised how far behind he was, she turned and waited, smiling encouragingly. She pushed a wisp of blonde hair that had escaped from her ponytail behind her ear, her head tilted to one side. His vision blurred again and he blinked trying to bring her to focus.

Was she smiling or frowning?

He couldn't tell.

He suddenly felt a rush of fear. He was as vulnerable as an upturned snail – and about as fast. How could he defend himself when he couldn't trust his senses? And what might he need to defend himself from?

Other than Mason, he'd been treated well by the people on Genesis III but the idea of something creeping insidiously through the station was unnerving.

How did he know he wasn't even now inhaling some poisonous, undetectable substance?

Or that this woman wasn't infectious, her breathe laden with deadly virus?

Or that something alien and invisible was attacking them all?

Get a grip! There'll be some perfectly rational explanation! Just deal with one problem at a time...

Jenner had turned and was still ahead of him, her pony tail swishing from side to side as she walked. She looked perfectly normal. If the conversation he'd overheard while he was coming round was correct and the first symptom was insomnia, Roscoe couldn't believe she had it. The baggy, white SES overalls couldn't hide the lithe body or the shapely legs. No one who'd been deprived of sleep could have such energy or poise. She was light on her feet, despite the heavy SES boots – like a dancer. The rhythmic motion of her long legs was mesmerising and he began to fantasise about being cast off in the shuttle with her, to take a circuitous route home.

'Are you okay?' Jenner had stopped abruptly again and turned. 'You look like you're not quite with it...'

'No, I'm fine!' He was shocked that his thoughts had been so inappropriate considering the predicament.

He seemed to be swinging between paranoia and fantasy.

She frowned slightly.

Her lips were full and he imagined pressing his mouth to hers and...

Focus! Roscoe told himself appalled that he couldn't seem to control his thoughts.

'You sure you're okay? I can slow down if you want. We're almost at the shuttle anyway,' she placed her hand on his arm. 'You may need to take it easy for a while. That sedative they gave you is nasty stuff. You may get headaches, nausea – even hallucinations. If you want to rest, just say...'

'I'm fine. Let's go,' he said more sharply than he'd intended, shrugging off the hand on his arm, whose touch – even through the course fabric of his SES overalls – was making his heart beat erratically.

She flinched and pulled her hand back quickly. For an instant, he saw fear and hurt in her eyes but before he could apologise, she'd turned and marched off.

Well, what had he expected? These people were living under the threat of something unseen, unexplained and unpredictable, which randomly seized individuals, turning them into angry madmen and even crazed murderers. And he'd just snapped at her kindness for no apparent reason, displaying the very behaviour that had preceded a slow and steady slide into insanity for a number of her colleagues. But if he apologised, how could he explain his totally inappropriate thoughts and the visions of her that had steamed up his brain?

Jenner stopped at the end of the corridor and waited for him.

'Open' she said and as he waited for the doors to draw apart, dreading the thought of entering the shuttle and seeing once again where so many of his friends had died, she grabbed him, placing her arm round his throat.

Roscoe struggled but in his current state, he was no match for her. She placed something cold to his temple and his knees collapsed as everything went black.

When Roscoe woke, he was lying on one of the berths in the shuttle and for a second, he thought the massacre on board and Jenner's attack had been a terrible, vivid dream. He swung his legs to the floor and sat up looking round for other members of the crew. Ahead of him Jenner was trying to prise open the door of a small cupboard and the realisation came that it had all been real.

He looked about but there was little evidence of the recent blood bath – just holes and pock marks in the seats and floor. Someone had taken pains to clean the shuttle thoroughly.

Before he could make sense of what had happened, she turned and smiled, tucking wisps of the blonde hair behind her ear, disarming him completely.

'Oh good, you look a lot better. Just relax a few minutes and you'll be back to normal. If Mason hadn't been so impatient, Dr Collier would've given you that shot in the sick bay. She told me to wait about ten minutes and then give it to you. Sorry about grabbing you like that but I thought you might not trust me enough to give you the shot. How are you now?' She peered into his eyes 'Head clearer?'

He nodded.

Should he trust her?

He didn't know but he certainly felt better now.

'How long was I out?'

'About half an hour. Long enough for Mason to call me. I told him you'd been taken sick again and we'd get the drugs to him as soon as we could. Any idea where they are? I couldn't find anything.'

'They're in that cupboard you were trying to open. Sarge had a key but he always kept it on him...' Roscoe broke off, fighting to keep the image of Sergeant Driscoll still restrained in his seat with his face blown away, from forming in his memory.

'The weapons are kept there,' Roscoe said, pointing at another larger door, 'I'll get a gun and blow the door off.' He pressed his palm against the detection plate and the door swung open.

'There's a gun missing!'

'Are you sure?' asked Jenner.

'Of course, I'm sure. Everyone on the shuttle had a weapon...'

'So someone on board Genesis III has taken it?' She sounded horrified and Roscoe wished he'd kept his thoughts to himself.

'Let's get the drugs and go.' Jenner glanced about nervously, 'Can you open the door with that?' she asked pointing at the gun in Roscoe's hand.

She backed away and placed her hands over her ears as Roscoe took aim.

He squeezed the trigger and swore softly.

'It's empty.' He jerked another gun from the rack, then a third. 'They're all empty! And the spare ammo's gone!'

'You mean someone's taken a gun and all the ammunition?' There was a note of hysteria in her voice.

'Sarge may have put the ammo in the other hold,' he lied.

There *was* no other hold. Someone had definitely stolen the ammunition. He could see faint bloody smears that still streaked the hand detection pad. It was hard to remember but he doubted anyone had had the chance to get to the weapons once Brazier had started shooting. Someone must have held the palm of a crew member to the detection pad after the bloodbath.

'So someone's taken an empty gun?' she asked.

He nodded confidently and she seemed satisfied.

'Well, there's only one thing for it,' said Roscoe, his stomach churning at the thought, 'if we want to get the drugs, we've got to find Sergeant Driscoll's body and get the key. D'you know where they'll have taken him?'

'Yes, bodies are stored in the cold room. They're kept there until SES sends a shuttle to take them back to Earth for cremation. I can show you…' she said, a look of horror on her face.

'Once we get the drugs, anyone affected can be treated and things'll go back to normal,' said Roscoe gently, seeing her reluctance.

'Only if the drugs work. And anyway, they'll only be treating symptoms. We don't know what's causing the problem in the first place.'

'But it's still worth a shot…'

Jenner nodded.

'I guess so. We don't really have a choice, do we?' She sighed. 'Okay, let's go.'

Whatever Jenner had given him seemed to have worked and Roscoe kept up with her easily now; grateful that his mind was more focused and his muscles stronger as the effects of the sedative relinquished their grip.

She led the way back to the central hub of the station and then out to Section Four, the production area where the bacterial vats constantly produced food for the three hundred or so people on board Genesis III, as well as generating the gases that were carefully mixed to replicate Earth's atmosphere.

'I hope they let you in, security's really tight. The fewer people allowed access, the less chance of contamination to the bacteria. Or that's the theory, anyway. If anything happens to the food or atmosphere, the station's in deep trouble – especially now our communication system's broken.'

As Jenner had feared, the technician on duty tried to block their way into the production area.

'Orders from Mason,' Jenner said briskly.

'No one told me...'

'Well, contact Mason then, but he'll be angry if you hold the soldier up, he's here on a special mission.'

The technician had obviously been on the wrong end of Mason's anger before. 'He'll need protective gear,' she said pointing to the packs of disposable hooded overalls, 'you know the rules, Jenner. Can't you go in alone?'

'No!' Jenner tore open the pack and handed Roscoe the protective clothing.

'He doesn't know where to go and I wouldn't know what to look for on my own.'

She pulled her overalls on, tucked her hair in the hood and led Roscoe by the arm into the production area. There was no way she was searching dead bodies on her own!

At first sight, the cold room gave no hint of the gruesome

contents stored within. It was completely empty, presumably to allow room for the large drawers to be opened. There were two rows of six, one above the other, each with a small monitor displaying the name of the occupant or in this case occupants as there were now 18 corpses on board – Floriano, Brazier, two other Genesis III members and fourteen soldiers.

Roscoe moved swiftly along the wall of drawers checking the information on the screens while Jenner hung back, hugging herself for warmth, her short sharp breaths enveloping her in water droplets that hung in the cold air.

'Anything?' she called through the swathes of mist.

'Are bodies stored anywhere else?' he asked pulling open one of the drawers.

She looked away.

'No, there's nowhere else.'

Jenner was grateful for the clouds of vapour that shrouded Roscoe as he unzipped the body bag and searched for the key. Finally, he grunted and pulled out a small pack of key cards. He briefly nodded his respect and slid the drawer home.

Jenner turned to go but Roscoe had started to pull out the drawer above Sergeant Driscoll's.

'What're you doing?' she asked, horrified. 'You've got the key, haven't you? What're you looking for?'

'I'm just checking...'

Roscoe opened and closed each drawer in turn.

'What for?' Jenner's teeth were now chattering.

'Get out!' The voice reverberated round the bare room, as icy as the chilled surfaces it ricocheted off.

Jenner and Roscoe swung round to see Mason standing at the door, his face a mask of fury.

'Move!' he ordered, 'You've no right to be in here.'

'You want the drugs, don't you, Sir?' asked Roscoe.

'They're not in here,' said Mason.

'No but the key is.' Roscoe held up the slim pack of key cards.

Mason scowled. 'I expect those drugs in the sick bay asap,' he said, standing aside to allow Jenner and Roscoe to pass.

He closed the door firmly and stood in front of it, with arms crossed, watching them leave.

'Jenner, I expect you to accompany the soldier to his quarters after he's delivered the drugs. And make sure he remains there.'

'You certainly rattled his cage,' said Jenner when they were out of earshot. 'What were you looking for?'

'Just checking,' said Roscoe vaguely. 'I can find my own way if you've got work to do...'

'You don't get rid of me as easily as that! If Mason finds out I've disobeyed him, I'll be in trouble. Sorry, Soldier, I'm coming with you.' There was a note of annoyance in her voice at his attempt to brush her off.

Roscoe needed some time back in the cold room. All the soldiers – or what was left of them – were in the drawers. He hadn't had time to identify everyone but each of the bodies he'd seen was dressed in military uniform except Brazier. So, where were the bodies of Floriano and the other two?

Mason had arrived just before he'd had a chance to check the last drawer but he was fairly certain it wasn't large enough to take three people.

'And you're certain that all bodies are kept in the cold room?' he tried again.

'Yes! I've told you! Is one of your friends missing? Is that it?'

No but three of yours are, he thought as he shook his head.

'Why are you so obsessed with dead people?'

'Just doing my job.'

'I thought you were supposed to be delivering drugs, not counting corpses,' she muttered as she let him into his quarters and left.

Roscoe rested for a while, until the sounds in the corridor died down, then he crept out of his room and made his way quickly to Section Four. He waited until the technician left and slipped into the cold room. As he'd suspected, there was no sign of Floriano and the other bodies.

Why was he so bothered?

After all, there was nothing he could do for Floriano or the others. But Mason's reaction to him looking at the bodies had been too extreme. It was as if he had something to hide. Roscoe had just closed the door of the cold room when he heard footsteps and he slid under one of the workstations out of sight. From his hiding place, he could see the SES-issue boots and uniform trousers of a member of the scientific staff. It could have been anyone but for the light step and dance-like gait.

Jenner! What was she doing here? Had she followed him?

She walked directly to the cold room and opening the door, she stepped inside.

How strange that having seemed squeamish before, she was now investigating the body drawers. Roscoe was listening so hard to the drawers opening and closing, he wasn't aware of the sound of footsteps approaching.

It was Mason.

He made straight for the open cold room door but before Roscoe could work out whether Jenner was expecting Mason or whether she was about to be in serious trouble, a single shot rang out.

Then three more.

He crept forward. Mason was a large man but Roscoe, although unarmed, was fit and well-trained. He had the element of surprise on his side too. But before he'd fully emerged, he realised the shot had been fired by a third person. And it wasn't Jenner who'd been the victim – it was Mason. Roscoe drew back into the shadows under the desk. Would Jenner come out and put herself in danger? He strained to hear but the only sound was the shuffling of the newcomer as he walked slowly towards the cold room door.

'Now you know, Mason,' he said, his voice slurred as if drunk, 'now you know that one man's meat is another man's poison. But you knew that already, didn't you?'

The man's arms hung limply by his sides as he shuffled away, the SES-issue gun dangling from his hand.

Roscoe waited until he could no longer hear the dragging footsteps and then ran to the cold room.

Jenner was crouching in the corner, her eyes wide. Roscoe held a finger to his lips, warning her to remain silent but she started to scream. Springing forward, he grabbed her and put his hand over her mouth as she began to struggle wildly.

'Be quiet! Mason's dead and the killer isn't far away!'

She stopped briefly, as if not sure what to believe.

Roscoe dragged her to the door and kicked it with his foot, revealing Mason lying in the middle of the room in a puddle of blood.

'You need to be quiet.'

She nodded her head and he took his hand away from her mouth but once he'd freed her, she backed away, looking from Roscoe to Mason.

'What are you doing here?' she whispered.

'I came to count bodies. What's your excuse?'

'I went to check on you in your room and when I

couldn't find you, I guessed where you'd be.'

'But you were checking the drawers; did you think I was in there?'

'No, when I saw you weren't here, I thought I'd try to find out what you're looking for.'

'We'd better report this,' Roscoe said sitting down at a workstation. 'What are your log on details?'

Out of the corner of his eye, he saw Jenner move towards the door and springing up, he managed to grab her before she escaped.

'What are you doing? There's a crazed gunman on the loose and all we know about him is that he's not here. So *here* is a pretty good place to be at present.'

'I'm not sure it is! You always seem to be around when people get shot. Perhaps Mason was right, perhaps it is you!'

Roscoe pointed at the bloody footprints on the floor, which led out of the room.

'Not mine,' he said and showed her the bottom of his boots.

'And anyway, what would I shoot people with?' He held his hands out palms up.

'You've got a gun!'

'And it's empty!'

'Well, p'raps you went back to the shuttle and got the ammo.'

'Jenner, I lied about there being a second hold. All the ammo has gone. I'm the only member of the shuttle crew alive and I haven't got it but I think I've just seen the man who has.'

'But you said…'

'I know what I said. I just didn't want to worry you.'

'Well, I'd say there's quite a lot to be worried about now!'

Before Roscoe could reply, a voice boomed out, 'Attention, all personnel, Emergency Conditions. Remain where you are. Security doors will now close until further notice. There is no cause for alarm. Keep calm. You will be kept informed.'

Metal slid against metal with surprising speed and the solid shutter slipped over the door, sealing them in, just as similar barriers locked in place throughout Genesis III.

'Wonder who's been locked in with the gunman,' Roscoe said and Jenner shuddered, her eyes following the bloody footprints to the shutter.

'I'll log on and get a message to Security about Mason. D'you think the killer will strike again? P'raps I can find out what's going on...,' she said.

'I'm going to check out the cold room again, in case I missed anything.'

'Will you please tell me why you're so obsessed with missing bodies?' she snapped.

'It's not the fact they're missing. It was Mason's reaction when he found us searching. Something's not right.'

'Nothing's right!' said Jenner. 'Nothing at all. And I can't get through to Security.' She stabbed furiously at the keyboard.

I guess I'll just have to leave a message. Did you get a look at the killer?'

'He was wearing a scientist's uniform. Average height, brown hair, very ordinary-looking. The only unusual thing about him was that when he spoke, his voice sounded slurred like he'd been drinking.'

'What did he say?'

'Something about one man's meat being another man's poison. It didn't make any sense.'

'Floriano was completely deranged just before he died.

69

P'raps whoever it is has the same condition. If only we knew what it was and what caused it.'

'You're a scientist; can't you do some more tests?'

'Like what? Mason tested all the bacterial vats. I saw the results. Everything was normal.'

'D'you trust his results?'

She paused for a second.

'Well, I did. But now, I don't trust anyone or anything. I guess I can repeat Mason's tests. It's not like we're going anywhere. Lock-down could last for hours.

Jenner had been moving back and forth between computers and machines that churned out graphs and sheets of figures for what seemed to Roscoe like hours, muttering to herself and making notes.

After being sick as the shuttle had landed, he hadn't wanted anything to eat but now, his stomach was churning with hunger.

'I'm starving!' said Roscoe. 'Is there anything to eat?'

'What?' she said absent-mindedly, running her finger across the row of a table of figures. 'No, sorry. This is a lab. No one eats in a lab. You won't find any food in here.'

'You got any results yet?' Roscoe was getting bored and he wanted to forget the gnawing hunger pains.

'I'm not sure. I think one of the machines is playing up. I've tried recalibrating it but I keep getting results that don't agree with Mason's.'

'What sort of results?'

'Well, it looks from these data like there's a contaminant in the bacterial vats. But it's not bacterial, viral or fungal. I can't identify it.'

'Could it be what's affected people?'

'I don't know. It's impossible to say without identifying it. But we all eat the same food, so it's unlikely to be the cause or we'd all be running round trying to kill each other.

'Perhaps some people are immune?'

'That's possible.'

'Is there any way you can work out what the contaminant is?'

'I've got the computer comparing it against every protein in its database but it'll probably take a while. If it's something completely new, I won't be able to identify it. Look, it started here,' she said, pointing to a massive peak on a chart. This shows the protein content of the food we produce in the bacterial vats. Then here and here, about three months later, there are two more huge spikes.'

'How do those dates compare to when Floriano was first ill? Is there evidence of contamination before his illness?'

'No, he died two days before that large increase, so the impurity couldn't have had anything to do with his death. These two other peaks occurred several months later. My results don't tally with the ones Mason published at all.'

'Where does he keep all his research results?'

'It's all held online but I don't have access to it.'

'Can we get to it somehow? How is it protected?'

'The identity pad will respond to his hand…'

Jenner shuddered. She'd avoided looking at Mason's lifeless body and the blood that had splattered up the wall.

'I'll do it,' said Roscoe.

Jenner busied herself with the results that were spewing out of one of the machines while Roscoe manoeuvred Mason so that he could press his palm against the pad.

'We're in,' said Roscoe has he dragged Mason into the cold room out of sight. He'd be in trouble when security finally reached them for disturbing a crime scene but he'd worry about that later.

Jenner's sharp intake of breath drew his attention back to the present.

'Mason's results agree with mine! They're nothing like the ones he published! See this line,' she said drawing her finger across the screen, tracing a red line. 'It shows the protein content of the food supply had been decreasing steadily over several weeks. At this point here, it wouldn't be sufficient to sustain human life. Then, suddenly, it increases significantly.'

'So, two days after Floriano died the protein content of the food increases?'

'Yes, so?'

Roscoe looked at her in silence.

'No!' she said slapping her hand on the desk, 'No! No! No! Just because we can't find a body... No!'

Roscoe remained silent. He hoped he was wrong but it was looking increasingly like the food produced in the bacterial vats had been nutritionally insufficient and Mason had found a way of boosting it by adding human protein.

'No,' Jenner said, 'you're wrong and I'm going to prove it!'

While she bustled about the lab, desperately trying to find the evidence that would prove Roscoe's suggestion wrong, he searched through Mason's computer files.

When he came across messages between Mason and somebody called Fisher, he knew he'd been correct although he didn't draw Jenner's attention to the fact. It was best that she'd thrown herself into work, thinking she could disprove his theory rather than having to come to terms with what Fisher had described in a strongly worded email as 'your abominable decision.'

Mason had defended his action stating that the lives of all the personnel on board were in jeopardy. The bacteria had behaved as expected at first and produced sufficient high quality food but gradually, they'd mutated or died. Mason had believed he would eventually be able to solve the problem but he'd delayed too long, stubbornly ignoring Fisher's advice to ask SES for help. And finally, he'd sabotaged the communication system in an attempt to buy himself time before SES realised he'd failed.

Roscoe had a feeling as he watched Jenner feverishly injecting samples into machines, scribbling notes and poring over charts, that she already knew the truth but would find it an insurmountable problem to accept. Despite feeling ravenous and slightly dizzy, he was now very relieved he hadn't eaten anything since he'd arrived.

Finally, Jenner sat down. She had her back to him but he could see her shoulders heave and he knew she was crying. He tried to comfort her but she shook him off angrily.

'Don't touch me! Ever since you arrived everything's fallen to pieces!'

He stood back, his hands dangling by his sides, not wanting to upset her further.

'I think you'd better read this,' he said finally, pointing to Mason's emails on the computer screen.

'How could he?' she finally asked, shaking her head, 'What kind of monster could go to such lengths to cover up a failure?'

Roscoe shrugged.

'But we still need to identify what's causing the sickness. All we know is that people started to become ill after Mason added Floriano to the food.'

As he'd hoped, the scientist in her took over.

'I've checked and cross-checked and the only difference in the food content was... human.' She shuddered.

'So why did they suffer the same symptoms as Floriano.

73

Could it be a coincidence?'

'It's possible. They may all have caught it from the same source but at different times. It just seems odd that Floriano was the only one to have it, then a few months later several people were affected. But the autopsy results didn't show any infectious agent – in any of the bodies. Until someone finds the cause, the whole station's at risk and we can't do anything about it except put ourselves into quarantine.'

Quarantine! Roscoe felt drained. The lack of food was sapping his strength and the thought of being trapped on this tiny outpost until he developed rapid onset dementia or was gunned down was almost too much to bear. He longed for his father's farm – for the sweeping landscapes that he'd once thought of as confinement. How little he'd known of life then.

Concentrate! He told himself. Solving the problem was the only way they could all escape. 'Could it be something in the air supply?' he asked.

'I've checked the data from the air and water over the last year. There's nothing abnormal. There's simply no obvious transmissible agent.'

Roscoe's eyelids began to droop. What was the point of struggling to keep alert?

'No obvious transmissible agent.' Her voice echoed round his brain becoming deeper and deeper until it was as if his father was speaking.

Suddenly, he woke with a jolt. 'No obvious transmissible agent!' he said 'We had an outbreak of a disease which affected the cattle on my father's farm…'

'Mm, well I don't think that's going to help in this instance.'

'The vet used those same words – 'no obvious transmissible agent'. It turned out to be Mad Cow Disease.

No virus, no bacterium, no fungus. Just some kind of weird protein.'

'Bovine Spongiform Encephalitis!' she gasped, 'Yes, yes, that fits. It could be. Those 'weird proteins' are called prions. If Floriano had a disease caused by prions and material from his body got into the food, Brazier and the others would have been exposed to them! And none of the results I've done so far would reflect that!'

She jumped up and hugged him.

'But what are prions?' he asked.

'They hijack normal proteins, turning them into rogue proteins which ultimately kill the body's cells.'

She searched for information on the computer.

'FFI!' she said 'That must be it. Look! It fits perfectly!'

'FF what?'

'Fatal Familial Insomnia. It's an extremely rare prion disease that interferes with sleep and leads to symptoms such as paranoia and ultimately, dementia, coma and death.'

'If it's so rare, how did it get on Genesis III?'

'It's a genetic disorder, affecting about forty families world-wide – that's only about a hundred people – but many of them come from Italy. Floriano was Italian and at a guess, he must have been carrying it when he came aboard.'

'Can you prove whether or not it's FFI?'

'Now I know what I'm looking for, yes, I think so.'

Roscoe watched Jenner checking data and injecting new samples into the machines.

Finally, she nodded. 'Yep, I've found prions in some of the samples.'

'That's great! Now we know what it is, we can get the right treatment!'

Jenner looked at him blankly and shook her head.

'There's no cure. Everyone who's eaten food produced on Genesis III since Mason added material from Floriano's body is at risk. Including me...'

The ever-present hum of the life support system suddenly ceased, with deafening stillness.

Roscoe made for the life support pod on the wall.

'Here' said Jenner pulling two life masks from her pocket 'I forgot to put these back in the sick bay.'

She handed one to Roscoe and placed the other over her face.

While Roscoe fumbled with the fastener, the lights dimmed, glowed brightly, then faded to blackness. Jenner reached out to grab him, 'Hold my hand,' she said, 'let's keep together.'

The lock down shutter whirred into life and rose, exposing the door.

'What's happening?' asked Roscoe.

'Safety feature. It's assumed that if the life support system fails, people can get to the escape craft. So the shutters are raised and we can move freely.'

'Including the gunman,' he said.

Jenner gripped his hand tightly.

'I don't think the escape craft can be used. They rely on the communication system working. If anyone's brave enough to launch, they'll be flying blind,' she whispered.

'The shuttle'll work but it can't carry everyone,' he said.

'P'raps we ought to get to it before someone works that out and leaves the rest of us behind...'

'No one can take the shuttle without Driscoll's key,' he said patting his pocket. 'How long is the life support system down usually?'

'This is only the second time since I've been on board. Earlier and now.'

'D'you want to hide out here and wait? It came back really quickly before.'

'I don't know. I'm afraid of running into that armed lunatic. We don't know who he is and we won't be able to see blood-stained boots in the dark. Even with the lights on our masks.'

'Can't we turn them off? There's no way we're going to be able to conceal ourselves looking like Christmas trees.'

'No, it's bioluminescence. P'raps we could cover them with something...

'Shh!' said Roscoe, pulling her down and pushing her under the workstation, 'Someone's coming.'

He shielded Jenner with his body and turned his face away from the approaching footsteps, to try to hide the lights on the mask.

Whoever it was didn't appear to be in a hurry and shuffled slowly into the lab.

'Come out, come out, wherever you are!' he said in a sing song voice that sent tremors through Jenner. Roscoe recognised the voice from earlier – it was the man who'd killed Mason.

'Oh yes, you're under the desk, like twinkling stars,' he said pleasantly as if they were playing a game of hide and seek. 'Now come out!' he barked, pressing the barrel of the gun into the back of Roscoe's skull.

'Ah, the soldier. And who else do we have?' he said as Roscoe and Jenner crawled out.

He raised the gun at Jenner.

'Your chance to run, Soldier,' he said, 'but she has to go.'

'No,' said Roscoe firmly, standing in front of Jenner, 'let's talk about this. There's no need for any more killing...'
He held his hands up, empty palms towards the gunman.

'You don't know what she's done. If you knew, you

77

wouldn't protect her. Stand back! It's an eye for an eye.' He began to laugh hysterically. 'It could have been an ear for an ear or a toe for a toe or pretty much any part of the body for any part! She's one of Mason's team and between them, they've condemned all of Genesis III to an agonising end. They used us as guinea pigs and now we're all doomed. On behalf of the crew, I've killed all Mason's team – except her. Now she's got to go!'

'I didn't know anything about it, Fisher, I swear! I've only just worked it out myself!' said Jenner.

'This isn't the way...' said Roscoe, 'let's just discuss this...'

'I didn't know anything about it!' Fisher spoke in a high pitched voice, mimicking Jenner, 'Of course you knew! There's no way Mason did that all on his own,' he snapped. His breathing was irregular and he swayed slightly. Beads of sweat broke out on his forehead and ran round the edge of his mask. They met at the bottom and dripped on to his heaving chest.

'Truly, Fisher! I've only just found out. If all of Mason's team had known, we wouldn't have eaten the food, would we?' said Jenner.

'But you didn't know there was anything wrong with Floriano. Not till people started to get sick. So why wouldn't you eat the same as the rest of us?'

'I swear I didn't know! I don't believe anyone else knew either.'

'Mason knew. That's why he sabotaged the communication system. He was hoping to go back to Earth with the shuttle and just disappear, leaving the rest of us up here to die. That's why Brazier killed the soldiers. He knew Mason wouldn't be able to get back to Earth on his own. Clever girl! You've attached yourself to the soldier to save your skin.'

'I didn't know anything about it!'

Roscoe moved slightly closer to Fisher, 'Look, put the gun down. We'll try to fix the communication system – there are computer parts on board the shuttle, then we can evacuate everyone from the station on the escape craft. There may be some treatment on Earth...'

'There's no one left to evacuate.'

'What d'you mean? What've you done?' whispered Jenner.

'Removed all the life support masks I could find, and switched the system off. There won't be anyone alive now.'

'No!' Jenner gasped, 'that's inhuman. People would have suffocated!'

'No, on the contrary, it was quite humane,' said Fisher. 'Wouldn't you prefer to go quickly rather than linger, exhausted but unable to sleep, nightmares coming while you're wide awake, knowing your mind is slowly shutting down – cell by cell...?'

He paused for breath and wiped the sweat from his forehead but inside the mask, he began to steam up.

Seizing Jenner's arm, Roscoe threw her sideways and flung himself at Fisher, forcing his arm up. The blow knocked the gun from his hand and it clattered to the floor, spinning to the corner of the lab, while Fisher sank to his knees, gasping for breath.

Roscoe kicked Fisher in the small of the back, launching him across the floor, grabbed the gun and seizing Jenner's hand, he dragged her from the lab.

They ran back to the central hub, then out along one of the limbs of Genesis III, to the shuttle, avoiding the bodies of people crumpled in heaps around empty life support pods.

Roscoe lay in his bunk, thinking.

The launch of the shuttle had been easier than he'd

anticipated and once clear of Genesis III, they'd found the food supplies, and contacted Earth, informing HQ of their estimated time of arrival.

It was going to take much longer to get back to Earth than normal – probably a month or so. One of Brazier's bullets had caused some damage and the shuttle could no longer fly at full speed. There were adequate supplies and under other circumstances, Roscoe would have been ecstatic. Hadn't he fantasised about being cast adrift in deep space with Jenner only hours ago?

But now he wasn't so sure.

'We'll need to take it in turns to man the controls,' Roscoe had told her, so we'll work in shifts. You sleep first and I'll wake you in three hours.'

'No, I'm fine. I'll take the first shift,' insisted Jenner, 'I couldn't sleep anyway.'

The Four Riders Of The ~~Apopalyese~~ Apocalypse

Every work place has a prankster and Heaven is no different.

Leonardo thought up the joke after reading the final book of the Bible, the *Revelation of John*, and decided that Fritz, the new Angel in the administration department, would be the perfect victim for his trick. It was inconceivable that Fritz would really send the advertisement to the magazine. In fact, Leonardo doubted he even had the ability to create such a document in the first place, much less work out how to email it to Earth.

Fritz didn't get on with the latest technology.

It wasn't so much that Fritz was technophobic.

No, it was more a case of technology being Fritzophobic.

No one could deny that he tried to embrace the latest hardware and software but everything he touched seemed to operate at best erratically, and at worst, with hostility.

After explaining that four new posts were to be created, Leonardo dictated the job advertisement to Fritz who scribbled feverishly in a notebook, using his own version of shorthand.

'Wanted.
Four Horse People of the Apocalypse.
No previous experience necessary.
Successful applicants must provide own mount.
Excellent salary and benefits.
You should have good inter-personal skills, be able to multi-task and work to deadlines within a team environment.

81

We are a non-discriminatory organisation; persons of any age, sex, race, ethnic or religious belief may apply. Flexible hours
Apply to George's Fish and Chippery.'

'Where's that?' asked Fritz as his hand skittered across the dog-eared notebook.

Leonardo had been quite taken aback at the question. He was certain Fritz would have worked out by now that the advert was all a bit of fun. It suddenly occurred to him that the new Angel might not be as stupid as he seemed. Perhaps he was pretending to go along with it all, turning the joke back on Leonardo. But the guileless expression and the tongue peeping out from the corner of Fritz's mouth as he furiously composed the shorthand note belied any form of intelligence, much less subterfuge.

'Shouldn't the applicants write directly to you?' asked Fritz as he formed the final full stop with a flourish.

Leonardo swung his head from left to right, as if checking for eavesdroppers. 'This is a top secret operation and there are certain protocols that have to be observed…' He nodded knowingly and tapped the side of his nose. 'Top secret,' he repeated.

'Top secret,' Fritz said enthusiastically 'yes, I understand.'

It just so happened that the eponymous George was an undercover Angel as well as proprietor of George's Fish and Chippery. The piscine eating establishment in Bentwood had won an award and Leonardo had read about it just that morning, so the address was fresh in his memory. He dictated while Fritz scribbled.

'No need to run the advertisement past Gabriel when you've finished,' said Leonardo 'it needs to go A.S.A.P. to the err…' he paused, trying to think up a fictitious magazine,

'...to the *Unicyclist Weekly*.'

Surely Fritz would spot the joke now!

'*Unicyclist Weekly*,' repeated Fritz, scribbling furiously 'yes, I've got that.'

Leonardo looked for a glimmer of realisation, but amazingly, Fritz hurried to his computer, ready to start the advert and patiently waited, staring at the blank screen. Leonardo watched him for a few seconds.

'I believe that you have to press here on the computer... and then here on the monitor before anything will happen, said Leonardo.

'I knew that,' said Fritz 'ummm, while you're here, perhaps you could just refresh my memory. Which program should I use to make this advert?'

Leonardo took control of the mouse and clicked on the icon on the desktop, launching the program.

'Oh yes, of course! Silly me!' said Fritz.

Leonardo left hastily before he exploded with giggles.

Fritz sat for some time, peering at his shorthand. The truth was that he didn't really do shorthand and although some of the squiggles before him were clear, others were completely indecipherable. It was lucky he had a relatively good memory.

He started:

Wanted.
Four...

'Four what?' Fritz muttered to himself, biting his fingernail anxiously. He remembered something about cycling and applicants needing their own mounts. But he was sure the advert wasn't asking for Four Cyclists. In the end, he settled on 'Riders'.

He carried on.

Wanted.
Four Riders of the Apopalycse.
No previous experience necessary.
Successful applicants will need their own mount.
You should be personally skilful and multi-task to deadlines within the environment.
We are a non-dislocatory organisation of persons.
You should be interested in age, sex, racing.
Ethnic or religious belief may apply. Flexible hours.
Excellent salary and benefits.
Applications to Award winning George's Fish and Chippery, 101, Hunter Road, Bentwood, Essex

He congratulated himself on remembering the address which had stuck in his mind since reading about George's Fish and Chippery winning an award that morning.

Several hours later, Leonardo passed the administration offices and curiosity drove him to peer round the door to see what Fritz was doing.

With tongue poking out of the side of his mouth, Fritz awkwardly manipulated the mouse.

'Aha!' he said triumphantly and looking up, he caught sight of Leonardo at the door.

'I've emailed the details. Would you like to see the advert?' he called proudly.

Leonardo couldn't resist.

He frowned as he peered at the screen.

'Apopalycse?'

Fritz looked closely at the screen.

'Oh dear. Well, at least I've got all the right letters,' he laughed nervously.

'Well, that's a blessing,' replied Leonardo 'where did you send it?'

'I couldn't find the email address for the *Unicycle*

Weekly but I did find *The Complete Cyclist Weekly – incorporating Tandems and Unicycles.'*

'And you sent it there?' asked Leonardo incredulously.

'Yes. And I emailed George of George's Fish and Chippery to ask him to forward any applications to me.'

Never mind, thought Leonardo. The editor of *The Complete Cyclist Weekly – incorporating Tandems and Unicycles* would undoubtedly assume the advert was the work of a lunatic and delete it immediately.

A week later, Leonardo received an email from Fritz, asking why George didn't know anything about applicants for the new posts. At least, that was what Leonardo assumed the email should have said. Fritz seemed to have pressed the send button before he'd finished typing the message.

Leonardo hastily contacted George, told him about the unexpectedly successful joke and asked him to play along. The whole set up had taken on a life of its own and Leonardo was keen to see where it would all lead. George was equally eager to see the outcome, once he'd been made aware of the possible entertainment value.

When the application letters arrived from George's Fish and Chippery, Leonardo was completely inundated with work on a special project, which Gabriel was closely supervising.

'Not now!' said Leonardo as Fritz approached his desk with the letters. Gabriel was expected in the office any second and he would not be happy if he knew about Leonardo's part in the spoof advert or the fact that one of the secret undercover Angels was participating in such a stupid prank.

Fritz's smile drooped and he hovered uncertainly by Leonardo's desk.

'Somebody will need to let the applicants know when

to come for interview,' he said reproachfully. 'You keep avoiding me. These people have been waiting for days to hear about their applications...'

'All right, all right,' snapped Leonardo, checking over Fritz's shoulder for Gabriel. And then he had a brainwave.

'Actually,' he said 'I forgot to tell you. You've been put in charge of this project, so you need to decide which of the applicants we're going to appoint. But there are to be no interviews. Okay? No interviews,' he repeated 'this is top secret.'

'No interviews, top secret' said Fritz. 'I understand. I'll draw up a shortlist immediately.'

His eyes sparkled with excitement.

It occurred to Leonardo that the joke had gone far enough.

'Fritz...'

'Ah, Leonardo, there you are,' said Gabriel as he bustled into the office, carrying a pile of bulging folders.

'Er, good luck, Fritz, I'll be in touch,' said Leonardo and promptly forgot the whole prank as Gabriel placed the enormous pile of work on his desk.

Fritz saluted; dropped two of the letters and head-butted the printer as he bent to retrieve them.

Clutching his head in one hand and the letters tightly to his chest with the other, he almost skipped back to his office. Leonardo had said he was 'in charge of this project' and his heart was nearly bursting with pride. It would be the most successful project ever – he would give it his all. Fritz had never had an opportunity like this although he wished that Leonardo had taken the time to explain exactly what 'this project' entailed.

Thankfully, the puddle of spilt coffee from the mug he'd knocked over didn't reach the letters and he mopped it up with the sleeve of his robe. He'd wash it out later. And it was also fortunate that the blood from his finger had merely dripped into his lap although exactly how he'd managed to twist the letter opener and stab his hand whilst slicing the envelope open, he wasn't sure.

Yes, it was definitely his lucky day.

He opened the other eight letters without further injury and started to read. When he got to the bottom of the pile, he selected two and dropped them in the waste paper basket.

'Time wasters,' he muttered.

He was definitely getting a feel for all this hiring and firing stuff although he reminded himself that he must exercise the utmost caution in making his final choice. It was, after all, a decision, which would affect people's lives, and the gravity of the situation sobered him somewhat.

Finally, four letters remained on the desk.

Fritz reread them.

Dear Sir or Madam

I am writing in response to your advert in The Complete Cyclist Weekly – incorporating Tandems and Unicycles.

I am a 61 year old, retired school cook and I would like to find a part time job. I trust that 'flexible hours' means that I could work part time, if I am successful. My hobbies include cooking, knitting and reading and as I am a woman, I am obviously good at multi-tasking, for example, I can read and knit at the same time and I dare say that I could manage something else as well, if pressed. I have a religious belief although I am not a regular churchgoer. I have my own mount. I am currently studying aromatherapy at evening classes.

I hope that you will consider my application for this very exciting post.
Warm regards,
Dorothy Miller

Fritz laid the letter to one side and read the next.

Dear Sir/Madam
My name is Oliver Fellowes and I would like to apply for the post advertised in the The Complete Cyclist Weekly – incorporating Tandems and Unicycles.
I am a retired bank manager and I am looking for a job that will offer me the opportunity to broaden my horizons. I am used to working under pressure and can work to a deadline if required. I am very keen on gardening and the environment and will be able to provide at least two references to confirm my skilfulness. I enjoy racing. I am Catholic although I do not regularly attend Mass, however, I would still consider that I have religious belief and could easily take up religion where I left off, if this is required.
I have my own mount.
Yours faithfully
Oliver Fellowes

Turning to the next one:

Dear Sir
Re: Advert in The Complete Cyclist Weekly – incorporating Tandems and Unicycles.
Name: Mervyn Roundacre
Age: 65
Occupation: Civil Servant although I am due to

retire from the Civil Service next week.

I like to keep occupied and would like to find a new job. I am used to working as part of a team and cope well with deadlines. In my spare time, I am a volunteer in an old people's home, and I believe that could be interpreted as having an interest in Age. I like racing and have been to the Royal Ascot Race Course once. I have ethnic and religious beliefs and will be happy to expand on my opinions if I am offered an interview.

I have my own mount and am looking forward to the opportunity to improve my fitness.

Yours faithfully
Mervyn Roundacre

Fritz picked up the final letter gingerly between finger and thumb. The corner of the scruffy page was slightly torn and the other corners were bent over.

Dear Sire

I wold like the job advertised in the bike magazine.

My name is Darren Howlett and I am 18. I have just left school and am looking 4 a intresting job. I am farely skilful but we had crap teachers at my school and my exam results were also crap. I am an intresting age and I like sex, hot rod racing and the Ethnics (I have all their albums). I'm not very religious but I do have half a GCSE in R.E.

Cheers
Darren

Darren didn't specify whether he had his own mount but if he was reading *The Complete Cyclist Weekly* –

incorporating Tandems and Unicycles, it seemed likely that he did.

After much deliberation, Fritz sent an email to George with the names and addresses of the successful applicants and asked him to write, informing them of their new appointments and inviting them to attend a meeting the following Monday. Surely by that time, Leonardo would send the job descriptions and some idea of the training that the new members of staff should receive.

Fritz sent the email six times to be sure George received the whole thing. Various people had complained that his emails arrived with only half the message, so he'd sent several of the emails to George in reverse order, with the final paragraph at the beginning, just in case.

At the same time that Fritz's emails with messages of varying order were busying their way through the Universe Wide Web, Leonardo's conscience prompted him to put a stop to the puerile joke once and for all. He composed an email, apologising for any inconvenience and explained that he'd been sure Fritz would see through the prank immediately. He hoped Fritz would forgive him and that there would be no hard feelings.

The message speeded unerringly to Fritz's email address and dropped straight into the Junk Folder, where it remained unopened for twenty-eight days before being flushed down the digital drain.

Fritz was beginning to panic. Leonardo was so busy working on Gabriel's project he was not answering his phone nor his emails and there were still no clear guidelines for the new employees. Research and some artful questioning of his colleagues, revealed a little about the Four Riders of the Apocalypse. He was very careful only to mention the topic tangentially in case he aroused suspicion

– this project was, after all, top secret and he knew how to observe confidentiality. He discovered that the original specification of the Four Riders was discussed in the *Book of Revelation of John*. Apparently, they were horsemen, rather than cyclists but times change, and whoever had sanctioned this project had obviously realised that in the light of human progress and development, horses are no longer the popular choice when it comes to travel.

Monday morning arrived and still there were no instructions, so Fritz decided to take matters into his own hands. He emailed George and attached a welcome and training document, which he had compiled, including the relevant passages from the *Book of Revelation of John*. Fritz felt embarrassed at not having more detailed instructions for George and hoped the undercover Angel's training had involved resourcefulness under adverse conditions.

He need not have worried. George emailed that evening with his report.

Hi Fritz,
    The Four Riders all arrived on time for the meeting and they got on very well together. I gave them your welcome and training pack and they read it during lunch. Who do I send the bill to, for the fish and chips? By the way, the young one had treble chips. You didn't mention a budget. Anyway, they have arranged to meet tomorrow morning at 9.00 am and I have asked them to regularly update me on their progress. I will forward all correspondence to you.
    Regards,
    George

Fritz breathed a sigh of relief. It all seemed to have gone

91

well although he wasn't sure who was going to pay for the fish and chips.

When Fritz started his computer on Wednesday morning, there was an email from Mervyn Roundacre, which George had forwarded.

Dear Mr Fritz,

I would like to take this opportunity on behalf of the other Riders and myself to thank you for appointing us to these newly created posts. This is most exciting although we are not completely sure what we should be doing. I'm certain that you will be informing us very soon of exactly what our jobs entail but in the meantime, we have organised ourselves and have started training. We began with some warm up exercises and then cycled two miles round Bentwood.

Oliver is a natural leader and he has taken charge. His time as a bank manager means that he is a bit bossy and he expects certain standards but he seems to talk a lot of sense.

The lovely Dot brought scones, which were very nice and she promised to make some rock cakes for tomorrow when we meet again for our training. She hasn't ridden a bike for a while but by the end of our session, she seemed to be getting the hang of it.

Thankfully, Darren is not deaf, as we all originally thought. It turns out he had those tiny earphones in his ears and was listening to his MP3 player while we were training. He has promised not to bring it tomorrow and is also going to try to borrow his brother's BMX bike, which will be easier for him to manoeuvre than the skate board he brought today.

I survived the training session although I'm going to be very saddle sore tomorrow. Still, I have quite a lot of weight to lose and I hope the cycling will help. I have also been voted in as the Riders' secretary, as I have a computer at home that works, so I will be sending in reports regularly.

I have been asked to put the following questions to you on behalf of the group:

Oliver would like to know if you are going to pay our salaries straight into the bank.

Dot would like to know if it's all right if she has Thursdays off, as she likes to prepare for her aromatherapy class in the evening.

Darren would like to know when the sex training starts and exactly what it entails.

I would like to know when the uniforms will arrive and whether you have outsized ones. Dot and I are slightly well-proportioned.

Yours truly

Mervyn

Fritz composed a long reply apologising for the lack of clear instruction and promised he would rectify this as soon as he could. In the meantime, he suggested they get to know each other and carry on with the fitness training. He would find out about where salaries were paid and yes, it was all right if Dot had Thursdays off. He wasn't sure about the exact training programme but he would get back to them soon although he doubted it would involve any sex.

Rather than say, yet again, that he didn't know about the project of which he was supposed to be in charge, he made an executive decision. There would be no uniforms, he informed them. This was a plain-clothes operation and they could wear whatever they liked.

93

At the end of the first week together, George forwarded the Riders' update, which had been compiled by Mervyn:

Dear Mr Fritz,

I hope you don't mind but we all took Thursday off.

However, we have been training hard and I have lost one pound in weight. Darren lost his MP3 player. We think it bounced out of his pocket when he took a rather tricky corner and came off his skateboard. And Oliver lost his temper. To be honest, Darren's language leaves a lot to be desired and Dot has insisted we use a swear box. Darren is filling it up quite quickly.

On a happier note, we are beginning to look the part. As the first Rider, Dot is supposed to have a white horse, a bow and a crown. She has painted her bike white and tied a large white bow to the handlebars. The only crown we could find was in the greetings card shop and is more of a tiara with flashing lights but Dot was quite taken with it. She certainly looks a picture.

Oliver is the second rider and luckily, his bike didn't need painting as it is already red. He has a plastic sword at the moment but has ordered a real one from a website on the Internet.

Darren was going to be the third Rider until he realised he'd have to carry a set of scales. Dot very kindly bought her kitchen scales in, but Darren told her what to do with them and we had to restrain her until she'd calmed down.

Oliver decided I would be the third Rider and I'm quite happy to paint my bike black and to carry Dot's scales although I find it hard riding with one hand.

Darren is now the fourth Rider and should have a pale horse. He says his brother won't let him paint the BMX and that silver is fairly pale, so that will have to do. He also likes being called Death. Apparently, his cousin is a Goth and Darren has borrowed his leather jacket which has 'Death' painted on the back. He quite looks the part.

*I wonder if you would settle a dispute, please? Dot has noticed that our initials can be made to spell out **DOOMED**. She says that it works like this:*

*__Do__ (t) __O__ (liver) __Me__ (rvyn) __D__ (arren). Oliver says that it's all rubbish. Either the first letters only are used, in which case it spells **DOMD**, which as he points out isn't a word or the first two letters are used in which case, it's **DOOLMEDA.***

Personally, I'm backing Dot. It can't be just chance that brought us all together. And Dot is such a very smart woman. She also gives a wonderful aromatherapy massage. Those oils are very soothing, especially after a hard training session.

Oliver has insisted that we all do a self-assessment but Dot and I think it may be a bit soon. Darren doesn't know what a self-assessment is – he thinks that one of us is going to do it for him.

I'll get back to you in a few days,
Regards,
Mervyn.

Fritz agonised over the reply. There was still no news about training or their objectives and as for the DOOMED question, how could he tell them they'd been picked completely at random? In the end, he decided to say he wasn't at liberty to divulge secret code words and leave the rest to their imagination. It wouldn't hurt to have a self-assessment on each of them and it would certainly keep them occupied, so he asked that they send him the reports as soon as possible. He was impressed by their inventiveness and requested a photograph of them with their props and their mounts although he didn't point out that Dot was supposed to be carrying an archer's bow, not a ribbon. It seemed heartless when she'd obviously put so much thought into her appearance.

Fritz was beginning to wonder if his email had arrived safely as he'd heard nothing from Mervyn for two and a half weeks. He decided he'd better email again and had just started to type, when he received two emails from George.

Dear Fritz,

I am really sorry to tell you this but the whole 'Riders of the Apocalypse' thing started out as a joke. I really think Leonardo has let this go on for too long. The Riders come every day and expect me to serve them fish and chips and to give them orders. I've had enough.

As soon as they come in later, I will tell them that the whole thing is a hoax. I'm really sorry but I can't afford to keep feeding them. They're scaring away my regular customers, especially the young Goth with 'Death' written on the back of his jacket.

I'm really sorry, Fritz but I thought it best to tell you now and not let this drag on any longer.

Yours
George

Fritz stared at the email in horror. His world began to crumble. How could this be? He'd put so much time and effort into this project.

And what about the Riders? What a blow this would be to them!

He clicked on George's second email anticipating even worse news. Obviously the Riders hadn't taken it well.

Hi Fritz,
The Riders didn't come into the restaurant today. However, I have just received the message below from Mervyn.
George

Dear Mr Fritz,
I'm sorry about the delay in writing this. I've been agonising over it for days but there is no kind way to say this and so I will not beat about the bush, I will come right out with it and I'll let you have it straight.
The Riders are resigning.
Oliver has got a job in a local garden centre and he starts on Monday. Dot and I have become quite close and have decided to take a short break together. We'll be touring Dorset and Devon on a tandem and then, who knows? Darren has discovered he is not ready for the world of hard work and has enrolled in a local college. He thinks he would like to take English GCSE and perhaps do the other half of his R.E. GCSE and make it a whole one.
I am so sorry to be the bearer of bad news and I trust that you will soon be able to replace us.
Regards,
Mervyn

The Way Of The Obtectus

The first suspicion that a change was imminent came late one evening after dinner. It had started inside Edgar Johnson's stomach with a faint fluttering, as delicate as the caress of a butterfly wing. For a second, he'd been tempted to dismiss it as indigestion and then as it began to increase in rhythm and intensity, he knew for sure that the Change was beginning.

Edgar was overjoyed. Wrinkled skin furrowed deeply on sunken cheeks as his thin lips pulled upwards into a triumphant smile. A string of saliva escaped, trickling downward, meandering through the grey stubble on his chin. Although time had lavished its trademark of sagging and wrinkling over the old man's face, it had failed to undermine the intelligent, penetrating eyes, which now shone brightly.

He'd waited so long for this.

Edgar remembered with pleasure his sturdy, virile body and the full and satisfying life he'd taken for granted but as old age had progressed, he'd become weak, weary and wasted. Blood still coursed through his veins but what he experienced each day couldn't be called 'life'. It could barely be considered 'existence' – no, his day-to-day experience was best described as 'endurance'.

But not for much longer.

A nurse bustled into his room without knocking, strode to the window in her sensible, flat shoes and briskly drew the curtains, closing out the dying rays of the sun. 'Cocoa, Mr Johnson?' she asked, without looking at him.

The bedridden man was silent.

'Cocoa, Mr Johnson?' she said louder, still failing to make eye contact as she fussed with his bedcovers, tucking him in so tightly that he could barely move.

Finally she looked at him.

'I heard you the first time,' he said 'but perhaps you'd do me the courtesy of looking me in the face when you address me.'

Edgar's hearing was no longer sufficiently acute to hear the soft click of her tongue but he saw the unmistakable movement of her mouth and the fleeting roll of her eyes.

'Would you like some cocoa, Mr Johnson?' she said slowly and deliberately, glaring at him.

'I rather think I might like some cocoa, please,' he said unhurriedly to aggravate her and as she turned to go, he added 'Nurse, would you kindly clean me up? I believe I've made rather a mess.'

'Mr Johnson, you need to call for a bedpan sooner rather than later,' she said, her lips thin and hard. 'I'll send someone,' she turned abruptly and swept out of the room.

He knew she wouldn't send anyone but it didn't matter. It was his way of annoying her. He didn't need changing at all – well not in the sense that she'd understood anyway. The change that he *did* need was total cellular renewal – and by the feel of it, he wouldn't have too long to wait. The frenzied biological activity inside his body was draining him of energy but he embraced the chaos, hoping desperately it wasn't too late and that he still had sufficient resources to produce the essential enzymes. He recognised the hormones streaming through his bloodstream but he knew that without the necessary raw materials, the metamorphosis would stop and he'd be imprisoned in this decrepit body until it drew its dying breath.

A different nurse brought the cocoa in and placed it on the tray in front of him. No matter that he was too weak now to reach out and take it – he hadn't wanted it anyway.

'Drink up, Mr Johnson or it'll get cold,' said the nurse as she left the room without a backward glance. She'd made no attempt to assist him. It was nearing the end of her shift and she'd merely been instructed to deliver cocoa, not to ensure that it was consumed. Edgar could see the drink was already cold by the wrinkly skin, which had formed on the top of the brown liquid. Never mind, Jocelyn would be in later to collect the mug and that was what mattered.

But he was thirsty. If only he could wet his parched lips. There would be no point swallowing the liquid, as he knew that his stomach was currently digesting itself and cocoa would be an unwelcome complication. He extended his hand to the mug but wherever the skin stretched as he moved, tiny fissures opened and began to weep straw-coloured lymph. Ignoring the pain as his skin cracked like shattered glass and oozed; he seized the mug and held it to his lips, allowing the cloying, brown liquid to moisten them slightly. He replaced the mug on the table with a grimace of pain that caused the wrinkles on his face to split, and then attempted to settle into a comfortable position. There would be no more movement now until the metamorphosis was complete. As the seconds passed, the cutaneous cells solidified, forming a rigid cuticle, which welded the lacerations in his skin together, staunching the now bloodstained lymph.

But as his exterior hardened, it was a very different story inside his body, where the organs and tissues were breaking down into a biological soup of individual cells and molecules. The only mobile part of him now was his eyes, which regularly consulted the clock on the wall and he mentally exerted as much influence over the destructive process as he could. It was important he didn't progress too far before Jocelyn came or he would be doomed to a new existence in this decaying body.

Of all the nurses, Jocelyn was the kindest, prettiest, friendliest and most importantly – the youngest. He'd spent hours worrying and hoping that when the change came, Jocelyn would be on duty and thankfully she was due to start very shortly. Metamorphosis always began spontaneously, so if Jocelyn hadn't been available for some reason, he'd have had to use one of the other nurses although the thought was quite abhorrent. Still, needs must...

Edgar strained his ears for sounds of Jocelyn's musical laughter, which usually preceded her. She had a wonderful sense of humour but he'd discovered her education was sadly lacking and she displayed a startling ignorance of fine art, classical music or literature. Theology, science and philosophy were concepts way beyond her understanding, but it didn't matter. Edgar had sufficient intelligence for both of them. No, what he needed from the girl was her youth. He lacked the vital spark that she possessed – but that would all change soon.

Finally, Jocelyn knocked at his door and entered with a trolley of empty mugs and plates.

'Mr Johnson,' she said in her singsong voice, 'you haven't touched your cocoa. Would you like me to get you a fresh one?' She had a delightful way of turning her head to one side as she spoke, like a sparrow. Edgar could no longer move his lips but inside his mouth, his tongue still retained some moisture allowing him to make noises.

'Are you all right, Mr Johnson? Can I help you?'

'Come closer,' he tried to say through motionless lips.

'I think I'd better call for help...' she said in alarm as she realised that he was unable to move. She suddenly became aware of the bedding, which was stained with blood and covered with large sheets of skin that curled up at the edges as they dried.

Edgar tried to shout 'No!' but only managed to make a raucous grunting sound.

With enormous concentration, he said 'Hold my hand,' through closed lips and implored her with his eyes.

Jocelyn reached for the alarm button which was lying beneath his hand and with a supreme effort, Edgar braced himself and slapped his hand palm down on top of hers. Pain, exhaustion and relief almost overwhelmed him as tears slipped over the smooth, inflexible surface of his cheeks.

Her eyes, which had expressed such compassion, now registered shock. The palm of his hand hadn't hardened like the rest of his body – on the contrary, it had softened and had almost begun to liquefy like his organs and as his hand came into contact with hers, they fused irreversibly.

She screamed, trying to pull away – a look of revulsion on her face. Unable to free herself, she stooped to retrieve the alarm, which had fallen to the floor but it had rolled under the bed beyond the grasp of her free hand. In panic, she desperately tried to drag the cable towards her with her foot, inadvertently kicking it out of reach.

She struggled against him, yelling and screaming and as a last resort, pounding his now rigid, carapace-like body with her free hand but within seconds, her skin, too, began to harden until she stood motionless and silent, bonded to the old man with terrified eyes that desperately sought a means of escape. No one had rushed to her aid when she'd shouted and screamed. The old lady in the adjoining room called out for hours at a time during the night and no one ever attended her, so Edgar, who'd anticipated Jocelyn's struggle, hadn't been unduly worried that his metamorphosis would be disturbed.

As the enzymes relentlessly ripped cell from adjacent cell, rupturing their membranes and spilling microscopic material into the cellular pool, Jocelyn and Edgar began to coalesce. Organic fragments mingled and before they both lost their identity entirely, Edgar tried to explain to Jocelyn what was happening – after all, it was only fair she knew why she'd been selected. His dissolving brain sought hers, and wordlessly, he managed to transfer his thoughts. It was important she understood before they became *One*. He told her she was privileged to have been chosen and explained that her youth, merged with his intellect and experience would culminate in the creation of a new and triumphant being – and it was all thanks to her.

Finally, the catabolism inside the two rigid human-shaped cases was complete. There was nothing more to break down and now the blend of cells and molecules began their period of synthesis – their anabolism. Hormones and enzymes orchestrated the entire procedure, using components from the rich, biotic soup, to create new tissues and organs until a vital, dynamic being began to materialise. After the rebirth of the body, there was a short period of dormancy while energy stores were replenished before the new life could begin. Finally, with enormous muscular effort, the body broke free of the solid outer covering, shattering it into tiny pieces and as it drew its first breath, its tender, delicate skin toughened on contact with the air.

The soft, dawn light was just beginning to filter through the thin curtains, casting indistinct shadows in the hospital room as the nurse began to tidy up. With disposable gloves, she picked up the fragments of tough, horny shell and deposited them in a plastic sack, securing it tightly and placing it with the other bags waiting to be incinerated. The bed was stripped, cleaned with disinfectant and remade in the precise manner that only a nurse can achieve. The single reminder of Edgar Johnson's occupation of the room was a small attaché case containing his belongings, which waited by the door.

The nurse picked up the case and without a backward

glance, slipped out of the room.

''Bye, Jocelyn. See you later,' called the nurse at the reception desk.

Jocelyn smiled and waved.

No, she wouldn't be seeing her colleague again.

Ever.

Not now she'd suddenly acquired the precious and unexpected gift of exceptional mental abilities and a wealth of memories and experience.

Edgar Johnson had made several errors of judgement. Firstly, he'd assumed his superior intellect would force Jocelyn's body to submit to him but he'd been unprepared for her vigorous and determined resistance, which had eventually compelled *him* to surrender. In fact, the struggle would never have occurred at all, if Edgar Johnson had not broken the cardinal rule.

Those who follow the Way of the Obtectus select a human subject with at least one desirable quality. The chosen human and the Obtectum are then merged to create a superior being, but it's the responsibility of the Obtectum to select an appropriate merge partner. Edgar Johnson had unwittingly chosen a fellow Obtectum and as a result, he'd lost his supremacy and he'd lost his life. And Jocelyn had unexpectedly won. She hadn't been ready for metamorphosis but the enforced cell renewal had moved her several steps up the evolutionary ladder that all Obtecta strive to climb. Now, with her superior intelligence and her young fresh body, she would experience a charmed life, such as she'd never dreamed possible. Perhaps she'd seek out a human with specialist knowledge of biochemistry and hormones as her next merge partner. An Obtectum who could control the exact timing of their metamorphosis would be master – or mistress of their own destiny. It was now within her grasp.

'Thank you, Mr Johnson,' she whispered as she dropped his attaché case into a rubbish bin.

In Need Of A Fairy Godmother

Aria dangled her legs over the windowsill and dropped into the night. She allowed herself to freefall, just for a few seconds, just for the fun of it, and then with a flick of her wings, she glided across the street. Hanging in the frosty air, she looked over the London rooftops and admired the twinkling lights.

It was just like a giant handful of jewels strewn on black velvet, she thought and then sighed, as she looked into the squalid street below. There were no jewels here. The darkness that smothered the dilapidated buildings was more like filthy rag, than black velvet. Wharf Street was a no-go area, although occasionally, someone, like the woman below, blundered in, and like a fly in a spider's web, they never found their way out.

The blonde woman staggered along on ludicrously high, stiletto heels. The tap-tap of her footsteps rang out in a staccato beat, too loud for this neighbourhood where people knew that the less attention they attracted, the more chance they had of reaching the end of the street alive. Even the rats crept silently through the shadows.

The woman steadied herself against a wall, tipped her head back and drained what was left in her vodka bottle.

She needs the protection of a fairy godmother, thought Aria.

As if to underline her vulnerability, the woman lurched forward, toppled off the kerb and fell on to her knees in the gutter, smashing the vodka bottle. She swore as several items from her handbag rolled into the road. Aria winced as the curses echoed off the stark, brick walls, and her sharp eyes peered through the gloom, searching for those who live on the other side of the shadows. As yet, they hadn't shown themselves, but she knew they would.

The woman was now sitting on the kerb, rummaging through her purse. She finally withdrew a handful of credit cards and banknotes.

'I'll get a cab,' she said loudly to no one.

Aria knew there would be no cab tonight, or indeed any night. How long would it take for the woman to realise she was wasting her time? But it didn't matter, the damage had been done. She was alone and incapacitated, and with credit cards and money in her hand, she'd demonstrated she was wealthy as well.

Aria sensed the movement before she saw the figure slip out from a darkened doorway and creep towards the woman.

She angled her wings and swooped down silently, skimming past his face – close enough to attract his attention but just out of reach. She hovered, hands on hips in front of him.

'Mine!' she said menacingly, keeping her voice deep and steady, 'The woman is mine!'

Eyes, from the depths of a dark hood, locked with hers.

Aria held her position in the air, ready to dart away if he was prepared to fight for the woman. Her heart was beating so loudly, she feared he would hear it, but he merely snarled, and turning, he slunk away.

The woman, who was now shouting loudly for a cab, had missed the moment of confrontation and Aria's victory, but others would have seen, and would be weighing up whether it was worth provoking a fairy to take her. They all understood the swift and brutal nature of violence, but magic... well, that was a different matter. Aria hovered above the woman in plain view of the countless eyes which she knew were watching.

'Mine!' she whispered fiercely into the night.

The woman's low cut dress and flimsy wrap were no protection against the night chill and she began to shiver, setting her sparkling earrings trembling and flashing. But it wasn't the jewels at the woman's ears that held Aria's gaze, it was the magnificent diamond choker at her neck which was surely worth a princess's ransom. How long would it be before the evil ones could no longer resist its draw? Aria needed to get the woman off the street and ideally up to her room.

Pausing beneath the light of the street lamp, the woman stabbed at the keypad of her mobile phone. Before she could make a call, it slipped from her unsteady fingers and skittered across the pavement towards an overflowing dustbin. It was still spinning when a foot extended out of the darkness and hooked it into the shadows out of reach of the woman who was on her knees, patting the ground frenziedly. A hand reached out from behind the bin and seized the woman's wrist, pulling her off balance, dragging her screaming into the blackness.

Aria hissed and flew into the gloom.

'She's mine!' she screamed, and flew directly at the assailant's eyes. He leapt backwards and there was a thud as his skull collided with the wall. He slithered, unconscious, to the floor and Aria grabbed his victim. There was no time to take the woman to her room; she had seconds to act before the predators closed in.

Aria had spotted her first and she was not prepared to share. Unsheathing her dagger, she thrust deeply at the woman's neck and with her blade buried to its hilt, she sliced sideways leaving a smile-shaped gash. Her frantic fingers clawed at the clasp on the diamond choker, slipping and slithering on blood that was pumping from the severed arteries. Finally, the necklace was free and Aria rose into the air with the diamonds dangling beneath her like a glitzy rope ladder. Figures appeared from nowhere and hands snatched at her but despite the added weight, she flew upwards into the night.

Splashing in the Trafalgar Square fountain was a shock – freezing but exhilarating. With the blood washed from her body and the diamonds, Aria felt lighter, as if she'd been reborn. Her life would now begin. The smallest gem in the choker would buy her a lavish lifestyle, the likes of which she had previously only dreamt, but first, she'd engage a minder, yes, the services of a fairy godmother were vital in the harsh reality of modern day London.

Solid As A Rock-Mate

Martin kicked viciously at the white pebbles. The resulting hill of stones created enough resistance to hamper the blow but it was sufficient to launch one single pebble which soared into the air, spinning majestically. It struck the tree trunk with a dull thud, ricocheted off the rough bark, landed on the path with a clatter, rolled until it lost momentum and finally came to rest against Martin's shoe.

If it were possible, Martin's shoulders slumped even more and he stooped to pick it up.

'You and me both, mate. We've both got the boot.'

He evened out the mound of pebbles that he had produced a few minutes earlier, spreading them about with his foot until they were level. If only he hadn't spent so much on having the garden landscaped...

But Lauren had wanted a 'labour-free' garden and this barren landscape of stone, gravel and paving was the result.

'You'll have so much more time to enjoy yourself when you get home from work,' Lauren had argued and eventually, she'd won him over.

Large sums of money had exchanged hands and he was now the proud owner of vast quantities of rock.

What a shame that he no longer had a job to come home from, he thought, and the prospect of hours of free time loomed menacingly ahead of him. The thought of mowing grass now seemed highly desirable.

He had been 'let go', 'released', 'made redundant'. It didn't matter which euphemism you used or how you dressed it up, he had been pushed out and the financial difficulties that he was facing were now insurmountable. If he didn't find a job soon, he and Lauren would have to think about moving out of this house with its stony, landscaped garden that had cost more than he cared to remember.

How could he tell Lauren? She had such plans for the house and she had even begun to refer pointedly to her 'biological clock'. Apparently, it was ticking and although it had taken him a while to work out what she was getting at, he now realized that she was hankering after a baby.

He couldn't tell her about the redundancy – at least, not yet. His father-in-law had been involved in a minor car crash and she had gone to stay with her parents for a few weeks. No, he definitely couldn't tell her yet. Perhaps, if he found another job quickly, he could avert disaster.

Still clutching the pebble, he opened the front door and made his way to the small, cramped room that he called *The Den*. He locked the door, yanked the curtains closed and sagged into the battered, leather chair at his desk.

It was no good hiding away from the world, staring blankly at his computer monitor; he needed to think – more than that, he needed to do something.

He placed the rock on the desk, turned the computer on and searched for his professional resume. A plan was forming.

There were a few details that he could add to the C.V. to update it but it was still pathetically inadequate. Still, it would have to do. He printed out six – reconsidered, and then printed out six more.

Now, where would he send them?

He registered on several websites, but it appeared that currently there was nothing suitable – at least, nothing with the sort of salary that he required.

It was time for Plan B.

Twenty minutes later, his worst fears had been confirmed. The rules had been established. Firstly, work colleagues and business contacts only want to know you when you are employed and therefore likely to be useful to them in the future. And secondly, there's no point attempting to recall favours because it doesn't matter who owes you a good turn. Favours, apparently, become null and void the minute that you are out of work.

Martin laid his head on his arms, closed his eyes and concentrated hard.

Thoughts and plans tumbled through his mind, jostling with each other for recognition and approval but there was no seminal moment, no blinding flash of inspiration.

One thing had occurred to him and he toyed with the possibility. If he were to die, Lauren would be able to use the life insurance money to safeguard the house but it would have to look like an accident. If the insurance company suspected suicide, they probably wouldn't pay and with the way that his luck was running at the moment, he'd probably screw up his own death and then Lauren would be left homeless, with a ticking biological clock… and no husband.

His stomach rumbled and he remembered that the last time he'd eaten, had been morning, before he left for work. A chocolate biscuit was all he'd had time to grab, and his stomach growled again, demanding food. Perhaps he could save money by cutting back on meals. It would do him good to lose a bit of weight; he'd noticed that his waist was getting rather flabby and a few days without food wouldn't do him any harm.

His stomach bellowed.

Martin opened his eyes a fraction and there, lying a few inches from his nose, was the pebble.

He'd had a pet rock once, many years ago when they'd been popular and he'd carried it around for luck. It had finally fallen out of his pocket when Billy Bryant had beaten him up one afternoon after school and he'd never seen it again. Neither had he bothered looking for it – what sort of good luck charm lets you get flattened by a bully?

He picked the pebble up and rolled it round in his hand, feeling its smoothness. There was a small lump on one side. Typical – he hadn't even bought smooth, regular pebbles. He'd paid a fortune for misshapen rocks.

He examined the protuberance and decided that it resembled a nose on a blank, white face. Taking a felt tip pen, he drew in two eyes then a smiling mouth and two small nostrils in the lump.

He surveyed his artwork and sighed miserably. The pupils appeared to be looking in different directions and one eye was larger than the other. The crooked mouth lay at a rather jaunty angle in relation to the other features, giving it a grotesque grimace or grin; depending on which angle it was viewed from.

Martin sighed and placed it on the desk.

Years ago, he remembered his grandfather painting tiny landscapes on pebbles that he had collected on the beach. Perhaps if he practised, he would be able to do something similar and sell them. Yes, he could start a business – he certainly had plenty of pebbles to practise on.

He groaned and laid his head back on his arms. He couldn't draw; neither could he paint and it wouldn't matter if he had a whole beach of pebbles in the garden, he'd never produce anything that anyone would want to buy.

Despite his gnawing stomach, Martin drifted off into a deep sleep. The room was stuffy and dark except for the desk lamp, whose light bulb bathed the sleeping man in a bright, yellow glow. What was there to keep awake for? Sleep was a blessed relief.

During the night, there was a series of power surges in the electrical supply – not serious enough to cut the electricity completely but sufficient to shut down the computer. The desk lamp, however, remained alight although after each surge, the bulb started to emit light of a slightly different colour. It was still faintly yellow but there was a greenish tinge now and from time to time, it flickered as if it were about to die.

Beneath its glare, the pebble lay motionless, gazing up to the bulb with one eye and observing the snoring man with the other, while it bathed in the strange yellow-green glow.

Hours later, Martin woke up. He was in the same position in which he had fallen asleep and his body was beginning to complain. His fingers were numb, his ear was folded over and his neck was so stiff that he was afraid to move but despite all these irritations, something else had woken him up.

There was a rhythmic drumming, which reverberated through the desk and penetrated his consciousness but it was the tapping on his arm, which alarmed him the most.

Slowly and painfully, he sat up and rubbed his neck with unfeeling fingers and blinked in the sickly-coloured light coming from the desk lamp.

It took several seconds for him to realize that the gentle thumping was coming from the pebble, as it rocked back and forth, alternately smiling and scowling.

Every so often, it hopped in the air, landing on the wooden desk with a thud.

Martin stared in disbelief.

A dancing pebble?

A gyrating rock?

He reached forward to pick it up and it skipped sideways, avoiding his grasp. Gently, he moved his hand towards the stone and swiftly grabbed it, stroking it gently, to stop it wriggling. To his amazement, it nestled into his hand, pulsating gently and purring.

Martin sat, stroking it until sunrise, his mind buzzing with questions and possibilities.

'How...?' he asked the rock, 'How can this be?'

But it simply purred contentedly in his hand.

At 8 o'clock, he decided to phone his brother-in-law.

'Hi Richard, how're you?'

'Okay,' came the guarded reply, 'how're you?' But it was clear from Richard's tone that he was dreading the answer. Richard worked for the same company and he'd obviously heard about Martin's redundancy.

'I'm fine.'

'You are?' asked Richard in surprise. 'Look, I'm really sorry about... well, you know... your job. It was really unfair. Morrison in Finance joined after you and he didn't get the push. It's not right.'

'Yeah, thanks,'

'If there's anything I can do...' said Richard although it was obvious that he was just being pleasant. There was nothing that he could do to get Martin's job back and as he was always broke, there would be no possibility of a loan.

'Well actually, there is something that you can do for me...' said Martin.

There was a pause and a guarded 'Yes?' Richard was anticipating a request that either he would be reluctant or unable to carry out.

'No one's going to listen to me at work...' he began, having come to the conclusion that Martin was going to ask him to help get his job back.

'No, it's nothing to do with work...'

'It's not?' The relief in Richard's voice was unmistakable. 'Well, how can I help?'

'You studied science when you were at school, didn't you?'

'Yes, why?'

'You were good at it, weren't you? You got the best marks in the year, didn't you?

'Yeah. Umm, Martin, have you been drinking?'

'It's 8 o'clock in the morning! Of course I haven't been drinking!'

'All right, all right. I was just asking. You're not making a lot of sense, you know.'

'I just want to ask you a few scientific questions.'

'Okay,' the guarded tone had crept back into his voice. 'What d'you want to know?'

'Do rocks ever move?'

'What, you mean like in rock falls?'

'No.'

'Continental drift? Plate tectonics?'

'I don't even know what they are.'

'Well what sort of movement do you mean? Give me a clue, will you,' he started to sound annoyed.

'Do rocks ever move about... on their own?'

There was a pause.

'When was the last time that you saw a rock get up and go for a stroll?'

'So are rocks dead. Are they completely inert?'

Richard considered for a moment.

'Do you remember Old Burnsy, the chemistry teacher?'

'Yes, wasn't he the guy with the bushy white eyebrows that he regularly used to singe with a Bunsen burner?'

'That's the one. Well, I remember him saying once that all matter is made up of atoms and each atom contains energy. He said that everything vibrated although some things vibrated so slowly that any movement was imperceptible. Perhaps rocks move so slowly that we just don't notice.'

'What sort of energy do they contain?'

'Martin, I don't know!' Richard was getting exasperated. 'Look, I've got to go; I've got a train to catch.

I can't tell you any more than that. If you want to know something else, you need to find a real scientist. Someone like a geologist…or a psychiatrist,' he added as he hung up.

Martin replaced the receiver and contemplated the purring pebble.

The phone rang out shrilly, making both Martin and the rock jump.

'Hi Babe, missing me?'

'Lauren! Err, yes, of course I'm missing you.'

'What's the matter? You sound a bit strange. Is everything okay?'

'Yes, of course. The phone made me jump, that's all. How's Pop?'

'He's doing fine, so I'll probably be coming home in a few weeks. I saw a beautiful fountain in the garden centre – it would look wonderful in our garden, just over by the…'

'No!'

'What do you mean, *no?* Are you sure you're all right? You sound a bit strange.'

'Yes, I'm fine. I just don't like fountains.'

'Since when? You've never mentioned that before.'

'I just don't like them, okay.'

'Okay. Well we'll talk about it when I get home.'

Over my dead body, thought Martin. There was no money available to splash around on unnecessary water features. He listened as she chattered on for a while grunting at what he hoped were the appropriate times.

'Well, I'd better go. Don't be late for work. Bye Babe, love you,' she'd finally said.

'Love you too.' He hung up.

He sighed. She'd be home soon and it wouldn't take her long to find out the truth about their financial situation.

'I need to make money,' he told the stone 'and I need to do it now.'

The pebble peered at him with one eye and gazed out of the window with the other, vibrating and purring gently in the palm of his hand.

How many other humans in the world were in possession of such a rock? In all likelihood, none. So, if this pebble was unique, thought Martin, it must be worth a fortune.

What would be worth more than one dancing pebble?

Obviously, it was lots of dancing pebbles.

Martin carefully placed the rock in the desk drawer – it wouldn't do if it escaped, or got lost – and he ran down to the front gate.

Until he understood which step or combination of steps were responsible for the transformation, he would have to replicate his actions exactly if he were to energize more of them.

He went out into the street and entered the gate – just as he had done when he'd returned home yesterday. A few paces up the path, he turned and kicked the pebbles, stubbing his toe. None of the rocks flew up into the air, let alone hit the tree. He picked one up and threw it at the trunk. It missed. He tried again. The pebble hit the trunk and dropped, not surprisingly, like the proverbial stone, and landed amongst the other pebbles. Martin picked up a handful and threw them.

'You all right, Martin?' called Harry from the neighbouring garden. He was leaning on the dividing fence, with a puzzled expression.

'Yep, fine thanks.'

'What're you up to?'

'Just doing a little gardening,' replied Martin, trying to isolate one of the stones and kick it against the tree.

'Never seen you do gardening in a shirt and tie,' Harry remarked.

'Harreee!' called a shrill voice from the house.

'Ah, the voice that must be obeyed. 'Scuse me. Sounds like I'm needed. See you later.'

Martin scooped up as many pebbles as he could hold and made for the house before Harry could return. If it turned out that striking the tree trunk and bouncing off was part of the process, he'd have to come out after dark and have another go.

Once in *The Den*, he laid all the pebbles down on the desktop, drew the curtains and turned on the desk lamp. The light bulb flickered but didn't go out. Martin breathed a sigh of relief. He didn't know where Lauren kept the spare bulbs, which was a shame, as there was definitely something wrong with this one. The light cast a greenish tinge over the pebbles, making them all look like they were coated in algae. Martin suddenly realized that he still had to draw faces on them and he seized the pen. His drawing improved slightly as he progressed through the batch and by the time that he'd finished the last one, he was beginning to get quite good at it.

Now what?

Yesterday, he'd fallen asleep next to the pebble but surely *he* wasn't part of the equation. Perhaps it had absorbed some of his energy? He began to feel rather uneasy. Had it drained him of something? Had it fed off him?

He opened the drawer, took the pebble out and inspected it. It shivered and whirred as if in appreciation of being handled and settled itself into the palm of his hand. No, he decided, there was nothing malevolent about this rock.

My Rock-Mate.

Yes! If he managed to make more of them, he would market them as 'Rock-Mates'. A whole realm of possibilities was just waiting to be explored. Rock-Mate clothes, Rock-Mate accessories...

In retrospect, he wasn't sure if it was the sickly green light or the fact that he hadn't eaten in more than twenty-four hours that was making him feel decidedly dizzy and rather sick. Either way, he thought that he'd better fix something to eat and then have a shower and change his clothes. If he had to go back into the garden for more pebbles, Harry wouldn't be so curious if he was wearing jeans.

He left the grinning pebbles staring upwards, basking in the ghastly green glow and went downstairs to the kitchen.

Lauren's shopping list stared accusingly at him from the kitchen table. She had made him promise that he would eat properly and had instructed him to get groceries each Monday. He'd forgotten, of course and now there was a very limited choice. The milk was lumpy and he heaved as the smell assaulted his nostrils. Finally, he found a piece of cheese and some coleslaw at the back of the fridge and wolfed them down.

Should he go and check on the pebbles?

He decided not to disturb them for several hours – no peeping and no interfering.

The cheese and coleslaw lay heavily on his stomach but the shower revived him and raised his spirits – he could hardly believe that he might be on the way to making a fortune!

Finally, he could contain himself no longer and he crept up the stairs to see how his experiment was progressing. As his eyes grew accustomed to the olive-coloured gloom, he could see the rocks on the desk. Silent and motionless.

He drew closer to the desk and inspected them carefully. Every so often, he thought that he saw a slight movement but after about ten minutes of close scrutiny, he had to admit that the results were extremely disappointing.

Perhaps they needed longer.

He decided to go to bed and possibly to stay there for the rest of his life.

Hours later, the phone rang.

'Hi Babe.'

It was Lauren.

'Hi,' he said with a thick, sleepy voice.

'Are you all right, Martin?'

'Yeah, I was asleep. I'm okay.'

'Asleep? It's only 6 o'clock. You got home from work early.'

'Yes, and I just nodded off,' he lied 'anyway, how are you?'

'I'm fine. You are eating properly, aren't you?'

'Of course.'

'I can always come home. Pop is a lot better.'

'No, no, I'm fine. Really. Stay a bit longer, I'm sure your Mum is glad to have you there.'

'Well, okay, if you're sure.' She sounded rather uncertain.

'Of course,' he insisted. The sooner she came home, the sooner he would have to tell her about losing his job.

'Well, I'd better go. 'Bye Babe. Love you. I'll see you soon,' she said.

'Love you too.'

He hung up with relief. At least he had a few days to try to sort things out.

Martin turned over, rearranged the pillow and pulled the duvet up round his ears – at least his troubles couldn't touch him while he was asleep. He drifted between sleep and wakefulness. Why couldn't he sleep? If only that dreadful knocking would stop. What was Harry doing? Hammering? Surely not at this time in the evening? And what was that humming sound?

121

He suddenly sat bolt upright in bed and flung the duvet to one side.

Humming and knocking?

It could mean only one thing.

He leapt from bed, raced to *The Den*, gently opened the door and peered inside.

The desk was alive with jostling, bouncing, grinning pebbles!

The original Rock-Mate was hopping about in the desk drawer and Martin picked it up, placing it with the other pebbles. It bumped and gyrated along with the others and joined in with the melodic warbling.

There was no time for sleep now. Martin set about marketing his Rock-Mates and replenishing his supply. He still wasn't sure exactly what the process was that transformed his pebbles into Rock-Mates but it didn't matter, so long as he followed the same procedure and generated more.

Lauren's father had suffered a slight heart attack and she had stayed on at her parents for longer than previously anticipated. By the time she returned, Martin had agreed some deals, which would allow him to clear most of his debts. He had sold several large batches of Rock-Mates to his local toyshop and they had almost walked off the shelves. The shopkeeper was desperate to buy more and word was getting round. Demand was outstripping supply and he'd even ordered more pebbles as the garden was starting to look rather sparse.

Lauren had been furious that he hadn't told her about the redundancy but she calmed down considerably when it became clear that he was now making large sums of money, without having to leave home in the morning.

'When the money comes in, you can have two fountains,' he had declared in a moment of generosity and her eyes had lit up.

'Oh, Martin, you're wonderful,' she said kissing him.

Disaster struck two months later.

He knew that something was wrong as he walked into *The Den* but it took him a few seconds to work out exactly what it was. At this time in the evening, the pebbles should have been vibrating and dancing on the desktop but they were motionless. They lay still, staring upwards at the bright, white light shining from the desk lamp.

'Lauren!' he screamed in horror, 'What happened to the desk lamp?'

She came running in panic.

'What's the matter? Why are you shouting?'

'The desk lamp, what happened to it?'

She looked at it with a puzzled expression. 'There's nothing wrong with it.'

'But it's not the same as it was,' he shouted.

'I changed the bulb. The other one was flickering and it was a dreadful green colour. Martin, what's the matter?'

'Where's the bulb? Where did you put it?'

'I threw it away.'

'You what?'

'Martin, what's the matter?' she said in bewilderment, as he shot down the stairs to the dustbin.

He should have known that his run of luck wouldn't last.

The bulb was broken and no amount of wishful thinking would revive it.

So, that was it.

No more Rock-Mates.

Ever.

123

What was he going to do now?

As the money had started to pour in, Lauren's list of 'essential' items for the house had grown exponentially and her spending frenzy had almost exhausted the profits.

At least he was no longer in debt but there was nothing for it, he would have to get a job.

Things could have been worse. They could have been a lot better too, he thought regretfully.

He opened the desk drawer. Inside, lying in a small cushioned box were two Rock-Mates. Martin had decided that he would always keep Lucky, the original Rock-Mate as a reminder of his brush with success and also because he genuinely felt affection for the little guy.

Lucky gazed up at Martin with one eye and peered at the Rock-Mate lying to his left, with the other.

'Don't be ridiculous;' said Lauren when she realized that he was keeping two Rock-Mates, 'they're not alive. They can't get lonely.'

But Martin wasn't convinced and uncharacteristically, he had opposed Lauren and insisted on keeping both Lucky and Peter.

Martin sighed and lifted the box on to the desktop, where he could see the two Rock-Mates.

He turned on the computer and opened his professional resumé.

Lucky and Peter purred and pulsated gently although it seemed to Martin that they were slightly louder than normal.

He turned the printer on and as it warmed up, the humming from the box increased in both pitch and volume.

Perhaps the printer is annoying them, he thought and he placed the box back in the drawer.

It was several minutes before Martin registered that the noise from the drawer had intensified but by the time that he got to the desk, the sound had stopped abruptly and he fumbled with the handle in panic.

The two Rock-Mates were lying side-by-side trilling gently but Martin's attention was neither on Lucky nor Peter, but on the six small pebbles that pirouetted and purred in the cushioned box.

The Rock-Mates had mated!

Martin screwed up the resumé that he had just printed and tossed it in the bin. There would be no need for a job now!

His fortune lay in a box in front of him grinning and grimacing.

Rock-Mates with ticking geological clocks and a hankering for Rock-Babies!

Henry's Box

Henry's life appeared to be a series of setbacks and disappointments. But surprisingly, Henry always smiled and told anyone who'd listen, 'Life is what you perceive it to be.'

'Yeah but wossat all mean when you get right down to it?' Bill asked dunking a biscuit in his tea.

'It's simple,' Henry replied patiently. His answer was word perfect after a lifetime of having shared his philosophy with friends and acquaintances.

'You can't stop bad things happening, but you can decide whether you're going to allow them to get you down.' He pushed the biscuit tin closer to his friend.

Bill's brow furrowed, 'Bad's bad,' he said, shaking his head, 'an' nothin' you can say is gonna convince me otherwise. You can't tell me losin' your 'ouse weren't bad.'

'Of course it was bad. But there's nothing I can do about so why dwell on it?' said Henry with a smile, 'I look for all the good things that have happened as a result of losing my home.'

'Like?'

'Well, like meeting you and the others in the hostel, for example. We have a laugh, don't we?'

'Yeah, we 'ave a chuckle now and again but if I could swap you lot for me own place, I'd do it in an 'eartbeat. No offence but if you can see the bright side after all the tough things you've been through, you need your 'ead read.'

Henry offered Bill another biscuit. He wasn't offended or indeed, surprised. Few people shared his views. But he couldn't imagine seeing life any other way.

His childhood had been so painful, he refused to talk about it and indeed, blocked most of the memories, but it had made him stronger and more resilient – better able to meet the difficulties of adulthood. He looked down at the misshapen hand in his lap. He'd been sure to use his normal hand to pass the biscuit tin to Bill – he suspected no one wanted to be served by a disfigured claw. He'd lost three fingers in an industrial accident, leaving only the forefinger and thumb, and that incident had been the catalyst that had propelled him towards his present predicament. And yet, he'd met every problem head on and chosen to view it in a positive light.

Take the work injury, for example. He'd retired early with a sizeable pay off which had allowed him to travel. Being very shy, Henry would probably never have married, but on a trip to Italy, he'd met Brenda and it hadn't taken her long to propose. When the money started to run out, Brenda had found a younger, richer man and had asked for a divorce, but Henry decided it was just as well. She'd been making his life miserable for some time and he dreaded the thought of spending his final years with her. She'd done him a favour by leaving.

Lonely evenings led to him seeking solace in a bottle of wine, then two, then… It was lucky the next door neighbour had come round to complain about the volume of the television. She'd spotted Henry through the window, sprawled on the floor in an alcohol-induced coma. After cutting out the drink he'd felt fitter and younger than ever. But the divorce settlement had been enormous, and gradually, he'd slipped into debt. However, the money problems made him more grateful to have a roof over his head – until that was removed, or more accurately, until he was removed from under the roof.

He'd found a derelict warehouse and spent a few weeks there in a dry and draught-free spot on the third floor. Wrapped in blankets and lying on old newspapers, it wasn't too cold at night although what he'd do when the summer was over, he wasn't quite sure. But a chance conversation with a stranger had resulted in him getting a room in a hostel for homeless men. How lucky was that?

From time to time, he went back to the warehouse, just to enjoy the peace. Many of the windows had been boarded up but here and there, brightness found its way in, illuminating the relentless grey. He sat thinking about life, as he watched the specks of dust suspended in the diffuse shafts of light. Then as the sun began to set, he'd take the deckchair down, lean it against the wall and make his way back to the hostel.

As autumn approached and the days shortened, Henry packed up earlier and earlier. He left through a well-concealed exit and increasingly, by the time he arrived back at the hostel, he was shivering and his fingers and toes were numb with cold.

Autumn gave way to winter and Henry wondered how much longer he would be able to enjoy his peaceful afternoons in the warehouse. People were beginning to notice that something had changed. When he'd asked if anyone wanted a sausage or potato from his dinner plate, Bill had always been happy to 'help' him out, but lately, Henry's appetite had disappeared altogether and Bill had suggested a visit to the doctor. Pete had offered him advice on stopping nose bleeds when he'd spotted Henry's blood-stained handkerchief, but it would only be a matter of time before people realised the blood was from his lungs, not his nose, and that the coughing fits were becoming more frequent. Henry imagined that transfer to a hospice would probably be arranged with all speed. After all, there was a long waiting list for beds in the hostel. His positive philosophy was beginning to fail him. What was the bright side of being packed off to a hospice to die? Henry had spent many afternoons in the warehouse pondering that question. In the end, he decided to wait and see. After all, it was impossible to establish the benefits of something you hadn't yet encountered, unless... he didn't encounter them at all. He sat erect in the deckchair, his mind whirring with ideas and possibilities. It was simple. He would take control. There was nothing he could do about his failing health and rapidly approaching death but it would be his decision where and when his life ended.

'Yes!' he said out loud, 'That's what I'll do.' His words echoed round the deserted warehouse, disturbing the pigeon who was nesting in the rafters. It flew out of a hole in the roof and Henry called after it, 'I'm going to escape too!'

The sun had almost disappeared by the time Henry scrambled out of the secret exit. He checked the size of the concealed hole. The box he would bring the next time he came, would have to be large enough for his purpose but small enough to fit through the opening.

'Where're you off to then?' asked Bill.

'To stay with an old friend in the country.'

'Very nice,' said Bill enviously, 'Whereabouts? Perhaps I might come an' visit.'

'Oh, it's a long way away,' said Henry evasively, 'in the middle of nowhere. You know you hate the countryside; you wouldn't like it at all.'

'I see,' said Bill indignantly, 'you're ashamed. You wouldn't want the likes o' me showing you up in front of your friend. Yeah, I get the picture.'

'No, Bill, it's not like that at all—'

'Course it is—' said Bill, stomping off.

'No, wait! I'll tell you but you've got to promise to keep it to yourself...'

'Right,' said Bill slowly, 'let me get this straight, you're not going to stay with a friend in the country, you're actually checking out because you're dying. You're going to that old warehouse, where you're gonna climb into a box and come out in a different world.'

'Roughly speaking.'

'An' what sort of world d'you think you're gonna find at the bottom of a cardboard box?'

'I told you, there'll be woods and trees and rivers...'

'How d'you know?'

'Because that's what I want. I'm going to imagine it and if I really believe it, they'll be there waiting for me.'

Bill paused. 'You know, if you didn't want me to visit, you only had to say.'

Bill avoided Henry over the following few days but it was probably just as well because Henry didn't need any further distractions. He was feeling so weak that he stayed in bed all day.

The following morning, Henry felt slightly better. If he was going to follow his plan, he had to do it while he was still able, so he placed his meagre belongings in the cardboard box and set off for the warehouse. He wanted to say goodbye to Bill and Pete but he couldn't find either of them and eventually, reluctantly, he decided he'd better go before his strength gave out completely. He carried the box to the warehouse and took his time climbing the dusty stairs, trying to catch his breath and resting on each landing. Finally, he reached the third floor, sank gratefully into the deckchair and closed his eyes. When he awoke, the sun had set and he wondered if he ought to have thought to bring a torch. But he decided he could probably manage without light. Very little exertion was needed to tip his belongings on the floor and place the empty box on his lap, yet even this amount of effort exhausted him and his breath came in short, sharp gasps. But there was very little to do now – well, very little that required physical energy. It was now up to his imagination to create a new world, and closing his eyes, he mentally projected a movie of flower-filled meadows and lush forests on to the inside of his eyelids.

Yes, he was ready. The scene he had conjured up was perfect. Henry laid the box on the floor on its side and with the last of his energy he lowered himself down beside it. Green light spilled out of the box and washed over him as he crawled inside.

'I got a bad feeling, that's all, Pete.'

Bill led the way through the warehouse.

''E always was a weirdo,' said Pete. 'Too cheery for my liking but 'e might just have gone and stayed with a friend, like 'e said.'

'Well then, there's no harm lookin', is there?' said Bill, 'And if 'e spent all 'is time up here, there might be something up here, worth being here for.'

'Like what?'

'I don't know but we'll find out.'

'And what if 'e did… you know… what if 'e's here and 'e's…' Pete whispered 'dead,' very quietly, 'it's been two weeks. It might not be pleasant…'

'I reckon we'll know by the smell…'

'I can't smell anything, can you?'

'No, only that sort o' musty smell you get in deserted buildings. Well, there's no sign of 'im down here. Shall we go up to the next floor?'

'I don't know…'

'Come on, we'll just have a little look…'

Their footsteps echoed up and down the stairwell.

'Wossa matter?' Pete asked, as Bill froze, ahead of him, one foot raised ready to step onto the first landing.

131

'There's a light on up there... an' I can hear rustling.'

'What sort o' rustling?'

'How do I know?' snapped Bill, half turning as if he'd changed his mind about going up, 'How many types 'o rustling are there?'

'Might be rats,' suggested Pete, 'or bats... and if the roof's collapsed, it'd be lighter up there... we don't 'ave to go up, you know.'

Bill hesitated, then resumed the climb. Reluctantly, Pete followed; the gap between them increased as he hung back.

'Blimey! Look at this... it's...' Bill's voice tailed off and Pete ran up the remaining steps.

Ahead of them hovered dozens of butterflies, their iridescent wings reflecting the emerald light which poured out of the box and bathed the room.

'Can you hear birds?' Pete whispered.

Bill nodded and looked upwards for signs of nests.

'They ain't up there,' said Pete, 'you'd hear them echoing. If you close your eyes, it's just like when you stand in the garden early in the morning. If I didn't know better, I'd say it was coming from that box.'

'Don't talk rubbish.'

'What's your explanation?'

'There's obviously a hole somewhere in the roof and it just sounds like the birds are close. It's probably where the moths got in.'

'Moths? They're butterflies, ain't they?'

'Not the right time of year for butterflies. But you'd expect moths in a moth-eaten place like this.'

'Yeah, s'pose...'

The butterflies dissolved into the green light and were gone.

'D'you see that?' Pete asked excitedly, 'they vanished into thin air!'

'They just flew off. Probably heard our voices. Stop imagining things.'

'S'pose. Well, shall we look in the box? I want to know what's lighting it up.'

'It's probably got a mirror in it or something and it's reflecting light from outside.'

'Yeah, probably.'

The emerald light faded and dimmed until all that remained was the grey, dust-filled gloom.

'See, just an empty box,' said Bill, kicking it over. He looked around, 'well, 'Enry was 'ere all right but he's obviously moved on now. Poor bloke. Don't s'pose we'll ever know what happened to 'im.'

'Nah,' agreed Pete as they turned to go.

When the echo of their footsteps had faded, green light began to stream out of the box once more and several butterflies shyly peeped out before fluttering upwards to dance in the light.

Most Precious

The high priestess knelt before the altar, holding the glass decanter to her lips. She breathed into it seven times; one breath for each of the goddesses she served, then she scooped up some sacred water, poured it into the glass vessel and replaced the stopper. Her life was ebbing fast and she wasn't sure she'd have sufficient strength to seal the decanter, let alone perform the dedication ceremony to the seven goddesses of the Heptadeity, but she would do her best. Most of her priestesses had succumbed to the Strangling Sickness and the few remaining members of the sect would follow soon – as would she. Heating a lump of beeswax to seal the bung in the glass vessel, she could hear the death throes of one of them even now. If only she had the strength to go to her sister and offer comfort, but she was too weak and she knew the sight of yet another woman wracked with fever, unable to breathe as if being strangled, would break her heart. She'd offered endless prayers of supplication to the seven goddesses but they had all been ignored and the death toll had risen, crushing her spirit and challenging her faith.

Had she displeased the Heptadeity?

She moved the spoon on which the beeswax was melting through the flame to heat it evenly. The weight of failure was unbearable, or perhaps it was just the final stages of the Strangling Sickness, squeezing the life out of her; forcing her to fight for each breath. She prayed for a speedy end for all her sisters. Their cave temple, hidden high in the mountain, was far from the city with its priests and doctors, so there would be no help. For years, there had been no contact with outsiders. Her sisters had fled the city for various reasons, but there was one common factor – each had been mistreated by a man – or men.

At a young age, she'd been forced into slavery but had

escaped and had led the others away with the promise of new life, certain that if they dedicated their lives to the seven goddesses, they would be safe.

But she'd been wrong.

The goddesses had not looked on the women with favour. Perhaps the man who'd once been her master, had been correct; men rightfully ruled the world.

She sighed. Soon, it wouldn't matter. They'd all be dead, hidden away in a remote cave, forgotten and unmourned. But at least no man could ever claim to have defeated her.

She sealed the glass vessel with the molten wax and placed it reverentially on the altar. Death would come soon; breath was rattling in her throat and she was struggling for air, but she was ready. Looking round, she saw the linen-wrapped bodies of those who'd already joined the seven goddesses, as well as those who were still half-alive, their chests heaving as they sucked in the thick cloying air that was already tainted with the stench of decay. There would be no one left to wrap her sisters or to pray over them when their struggle was over.

She raised her eyes to the altar. Unlike other temples, there was no gold or precious stones; everything used in their worship had been made from natural materials like wood or stone – all except the glass decanter. She'd smuggled it from the city when she'd fled, although it was doubtful that anyone would have missed such a simple item. It could not be described as beautiful, but now, because of its contents, it had become most precious. It contained an offering of sacred water and her last breaths. Without water and air there was no life, so what greater gift could she offer the seven goddesses she served?

The field trip had been a disaster – until now. The students had criticised the food, the accommodation, the lack of wifi and above all, the weather, which according to the locals, hadn't been this bad for years. It had rained incessantly, transforming the archaeological digs into mud baths and had sorely tried Dr Andrew Paynton's patience, but he had every reason to thank the weather now.

The pickup truck carrying him and senior scientist, Dr Diana Knowsley, had run out of petrol half way to a dig site and the driver had set off down a mountain path with a jerry can, promising to hurry back. Two hours later, he hadn't returned and Diana was worried they wouldn't make it back to the hostel before nightfall. Stupid hysterical woman! There was no point moaning at him. It wasn't his fault a sudden storm had blown up, nor that the driver had taken the truck keys, leaving them with no shelter.

He'd suggested they search the rock face for an overhanging ledge under which to shelter from the deluge, and that's when he'd lost his footing on a mossy boulder and his leg had slipped down a crack, dislodging an avalanche of rocks. Once he'd pulled his leg out, he'd realised he'd found a blocked-up entrance to a cave and breathless with excitement, he'd removed stones until the hole was large enough for him to squeeze into. Before Diana could object, he'd begun to inch along the narrow tunnel into the main cavern, lighting his way with a torch. She'd wanted to join him but he'd pointed out that she needed to remain outside in case he needed help, as well as to keep watch for the driver. When she began to argue, he simply ignored her and carried on crawling along the tunnel.

Dr Paynton hardly dared to breath; everywhere his torch beam alighted, wonderful things came into view. As well as urns and statues, there were dozens of skeletons on the ground. Some had been laid on their backs with hands folded on their chests, but others were in the foetal position as if they had died in pain and been abandoned without a death ceremony. To his left was what looked like a large, stone altar covered with artefacts. On the steps leading to the altar was a skeleton – from the shape of the pelvis, he was certain it was that of a female – and she appeared to be lying as if in prayer; face down, with her arms outstretched.

'What can you see?' Diana called.

'Nothing,' he replied. He'd take as many photographs as he could and tonight in front of the members of his university department, he'd produce his evidence and claim the find as his own. Diana would know he'd double-crossed her, but so what? After years of professional anonymity, he would have the recognition he deserved and would no longer take second place, to a second rate woman.

All the skeletons he'd observed so far, appeared to have belonged to women, which made this discovery quite remarkable. As far as he knew, there was no historical evidence for a community of cave-dwellers in this area, let alone what might turn out to be a secret women's cult.

'Are you all right?' Diana called.

'I'm fine. Just lost my lens cap. Won't be long...'

Heading towards the altar, his torch beam spilled over on to the wall behind the flat-topped rock, illuminating an enormous mural, and he froze, the hairs on the back of his neck, prickling. This was no primitive cave art. In fact, he'd never seen anything so exquisite. The artist had skilfully painted seven life-sized female dancers, their long tunics swirling as they moved but even more exciting than the figures, were the hieroglyphs below their feet. Surely the writing would tell him who these women were and what they were doing here. Very few of the markings were familiar, and he wondered if he'd stumbled upon a new language. He clicked repeatedly with his camera, recording the frieze and hieroglyphs, trying to keep his trembling hands steady and cursing as the batteries began to fail.

137

He was sure this was an extremely important find – perhaps unique – but he couldn't help being disappointed that there were no jewels or precious metals. Mostly, the items were stone or clay, all except a rather unremarkable – almost ugly – glass vessel on the altar. Nevertheless, he reminded himself, it wasn't the value of the individual pieces that was important but the entire site which was of inestimable significance.

'Dr Diana Knowsley,' he said aloud, 'eat your heart out.'

Heart out... heart out... out... out... came the reply from the cave.

Diana's shouts and the clatter of rocks falling, warned him it was time to leave. He patted the camera in his chest pocket. There was enough evidence in it to ensure his place in history.

The spirit of the high priestess stirred in the darkness. She alone had remained in the temple, her sisters' souls having slipped away one by one, to the protection of the Heptadeity, but she'd refused to leave. For centuries, she'd remained quiescent in the darkness, secure in the belief their tomb was sealed, but now, she watched the man who'd defiled her holy place with his presence. She was consumed with rage by her impotence in the face of such desecration. Her body had been too weak to defend itself when she was alive, and now her spirit was even more powerless. Nothing had changed over the centuries; men still ruled the world.

She flinched as light flashed from the box he was holding in his hands, lighting up the painting of the seven goddesses. Never before, had the dancing figures been witnessed by a man, and she wanted to scream her outrage at the sacrilege. So far, he hadn't touched anything but now, he moved purposefully to the altar, stepping over the remains of what had once been her body, and inspecting the altar goods.

She willed him not to touch the glass decanter but she knew he would. A man from the future would be sophisticated enough to identify the most precious item in the cave temple. Sure enough, he picked it up and she heard the almost imperceptible sound of the wax that had once sealed the stopper, crack and break. The man lifted the plug and gingerly sniffed the contents of the vessel, his face registering nothing.

Foolish man! The sacred water would evaporate now the seal was broken and as for her seven breaths, they'd been destroyed. He'd consumed them, breathing them in, overpowering them with his living breath and incorporating them into his body.

They were hers no more.

Her life and death had been a series of meaningless events, over which she'd had no control.

'How could you allow this?' she screamed to the seven goddesses.

She didn't expect them to respond, after all, they'd been absent from the temple for centuries, but out of the silence, she heard the merest whisper which grew until it was like a rushing wind; 'We have seen your devotion and understand your needs. You have been heard.'

Their words spun round her, lifting her up and bearing her out of the tomb. Below, she saw a woman drag the motionless man out of the cave entrance to the road, seconds before the tunnel collapsed.

He was unconscious and the woman placed her fingers on his neck, then put her mouth over his and blew. His chest inflated and after a few moments, he opened his eyes. The woman looked up and down the road, as if looking for something, despair on her face.

So, the man was alive. Disappointment washed over the high priestess.

'Look closer,' whispered the goddesses.

In his chest pocket, she could see the light-box he'd pointed at so many items in the temple. It was smashed and broken.

'Look deeper,' the goddesses whispered.

She could see her breaths inside his body and within them, tiny grains of life, that she had no words to describe, were germinating inside him, sending out growths, like roots, taking over his living tissue. She knew that soon, he would struggle to breathe, just as she and her sisters had, and that in a short time, he would surrender to the Strangling Sickness.

Her sanctuary was secure; this man would not live long enough to tell what he had seen.

Her final breaths had not been in vain.

Other Books by Dawn Knox

The Great War

100 stories of 100 words honouring those who lived and died 100 years Ago.

"I love this book. What an interesting and 'novel' way to write about so many different people's experiences. I have dipped in and out, back and forth a number of times. It certainly lends itself to re reading. Highly recommended." (*Amazon*)

Aavailable from Amazon:

Paperback: ISBN 978-1-532961-59-5
http://www.hyperurl.co/yi8aah

eBook: ASIN B01FFRN7FW
http://www.hyperurl.co/d39nko

Daffodil and the Thin Place

A book for children or young teens

One simple yawn is all it takes for teenager Daffodil
Lane to unknowingly breathe in a wandering soul and
swallow it, trapping it in her stomach. To the rest of the
world, the soul sounds like a rumbling tummy, but
horrified Daffodil hears a voice insistently demanding to
be released. She travels back in time more than 100 years
in an attempt to rid herself of the voice and to reunite it
with its body, but the repercussions of her journey
reverberate through the years, affecting the lives of
people in both the Victorian times and the 21st Century.

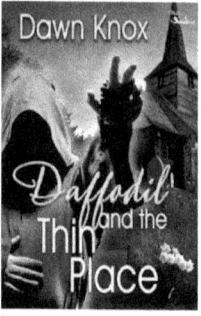

"A brilliant writer and story - I could not put it down
until I had finished it but at the same time did not want it
to end!" (*Amazon*)

Aavailable from Amazon:

Paperback: ISBN 978-1-514367-42-1
http://www.hyperurl.co/xkd4o0

eBook: ASIN B00L3CVX1E
http://www.hyperurl.co/m7jr3z

Other Publications by Bridge House

Snowflakes

edited by Debz Hobbs-Wyatt and Gill James

Our theme for 2015 is snowflakes. Stories that contain
snowflakes and that are like snowflakes. Unique and
perfectly formed. As they melt into the psyche they bring a
life-sustaining force. Snow can be beautiful and it can be
treacherous. It can swing from one extreme to another in
seconds. It is an important part of the nature cycle. Here you
will find that our writers have risen to the challenge.

"Great collection of fresh, innovative and moving stories. Best
read near a roaring fire, as some of the stories are chilling
indeed. Highly recommended" (*Amazon*)

Order from www.bridgehousepublishing.co.uk

Paperback: ISBN 978-1-907335-40-2
eBook: ISBN 978-1-907335-41-9

Baubles

edited by Debz Hobbs-Wyatt and Gill James

The challenge was to write a bauble of a story. So we have a
varied selection of snippets that sparkle. Once again we feel
privileged to publish this fine group of writers. Each story is
different and glitters in its own way.

Order from www.bridgehousepublishing.co.uk

Paperback: ISBN 978-1-907335-46-4
eBook: ISBN 978-1-907335-47-1